THE MOORLANDERS

THE
MOORLANDERS

STEVEN D COLES

Matador
9 Priory Business Park,
Wistow Road, Kibworth Beauchamp,
Leicestershire LE8 0RX
Tel: 0116 279 2299
Email: books@troubador.co.uk
Web: www.troubador.co.uk/matador
Twitter: @matadorbooks

ISBN 978 1 83859 478 7

British Library Cataloguing in Publication Data.
A catalogue record for this book is available from the British Library.

Printed and bound in Great Britain by 4edge Limited
Typeset in 11pt Baskerville by Troubador Publishing Ltd, Leicester, UK

Matador is an imprint of Troubador Publishing Ltd

For my boys
Damien, Ed, Tom, Brendan and Arthur.

My profound thanks to-
My mother for her meticulous grammatical edits
And to Helen for her endless patience in
unravelling my IT disasters

CONTENTS

Hanging Stone Hill
(Seat of the Lord of the North Moor)

DARTMOOR

7

Crow Tor

Grimspound

Wistman's
Wood

Bowermans
Nose

The
Great River

Fox Tor
Mire

Sheeps
Tor

Drizzlecombe

Blackdown
Rings

6

N

W   E

S

1

2

Buzzard
Woods

3

4

5

The Sea

DESIGNATION OF RIVERS	MODERN NAMES
Great River	Tamar
First River	Meavy
Second River	Plym
Third River	Yealm
Fourth River	Erme
Fifth River	Avon
Sixth River	Dart
Seventh River	Teign

LIST OF MAIN CHARACTERS

Moorlanders of Buzzard Woods

Caradoc Courageous and endlessly inquisitive.

Rollo
Michaelmas
Piebald Friends of Caradoc
NarWhal
Polycanthus

Arken Caradoc's Father

Hama His friend

Dogstooth Brother of Hama

Bluffinch Caradoc's rival and eventual friend

Granny Grizabelle Venerable old lady

Gorbaduc Buzzard Woods Chef and brewer of Corma Beer

Berengaria Young Moorlander reowned for her powers of sarcasm

Elders of Moorlander Marks

Ebenezer   Elder of Buzzard Woods

Potentilla   Elder of Sheepstor Mark and
                      skilled herbalist

Ambergris   Elder of Grimspound and
                      the Senior Elder

Fortinbras   Elder of Drizzlecombe

Badgers of Buzzard Woods

Hamilcar

Hasdrubal

Moorlanders from other Marks

Fontanella (Ellie)   Young Moorlander from Drizzlecombe
                         - selected by Findhorn to accompany
                         Caradoc on his most perilous journey

Imogen   Caradoc's Mother

Hyperica   Friend of Caradoc's Mother.
                      Skilled Archer

Turmeric	Brother of Ebenezer sometime prisoner of Lord of the Northmoor
Lemuella	Member of patrol to Northmoors. Skilled Archer
Romulus	Moorlander taken by Hydrax the Cave Bear
Lungwort **Cloudberry** **Dogberry**	Young Moorlanders of Drizzlecombe who accompany Caradoc to Vixen Tor
Brand	Father of Ellie and Moorlander Warrior

Non-Moorlander Characters

Findhorn	A Mage
Bowerman	Legendary Moorland Giant
Wolfsbane	Leader of the Mercenary Badgers
Vixana	A Witch
Magog	The Sorcerer
Wistman	The Lord of the Northmoor

CHAPTER ONE

THE ESCAPE

Horns blew wildly over Saddlemoor Down. The sound of harsh voices disturbed the tranquil evening, and a few sheep grazing peacefully on the grassy slopes raised their heads, looked towards the din and moved uneasily off towards the open moor.

From behind a rocky promontory two small figures came scampering. They moved with surprising speed downhill in the direction of a thickly wooded valley, some 150 metres away. The horns sounded again and with them came the thunder of galloping hooves. The two figures paused and looked back. A third figure emerged from behind the rocks, portlier than the others and less agile. It staggered a few paces then stumbled and fell.

"Come on, Rollo, hurry, they'll catch you," called the larger of the two. Rollo raised his head and staggered, half running, half crawling, after them. His companions waited briefly for him to catch up. Then, each took hold of a shoulder and between them they propelled the grateful Rollo downhill towards the woods.

The three young Moorlanders, for such they were, had covered a further thirty or forty metres when the cause of their panic came into view. Around the rocky promontory galloped a large black stallion, followed immediately by three others. Each horse carried a man-sized figure. Each figure wore a heavy mask which completely obscured its face. The four riders halted, and their leader raised his head and seemed to gaze intently in the direction of the fleeing figures. A thin piercing cry like that of a screech owl oozed from beneath the mask, and immediately the four horses reared and galloped forward in hot pursuit.

They gained on the Moorlanders so quickly that escape into the warm, welcoming woods seemed impossible. In spite of their name, the Moorlanders are at home in the wooded moorland river valleys rather than on the open moor, and they knew that their only hope lay in reaching the safety of the trees, where the horses could not gallop, before they were overtaken. But at this moment the borders of the wood contained more than trees. Five pairs of eyes peered out from between the lowest branches and watched the chase with alarm.

The three Moorlanders were still some distance from the first trees when the leader of their pursuers, now closing on them fast, uttered a second cry, crow-like and harsh. In reply, each rider raised a vicious curved sword and held it aloft. Their leader brandished a huge many-pointed mace, waved it twice around his head and spurred his mount toward the hindmost Moorlander. The gap between the two had closed to a few yards when the leader's progress was ended abruptly. His horse gave a shrill cry, reared its forehooves and collapsed sideways. Its rider was thrown headlong into the path of the following horse and pummelled beneath its hooves. The third horse's desperate attempts to avoid the mele were to no avail, and a tangled mass of flailing hooves, manes, bodies and weaponry ensued. A single horse alone escaped the confusion. The black stallion lay apart from the rest, lifeless, slain by a single arrow embedded in its throat.

The three Moorlanders wasted little time in surveying the misfortunes of their pursuers. They suspected, but had not seen the cause of, their deliverance. They continued their flight on towards the safety of the woodland, and soon passed under the protective shadow of the first trees and scurried on into the thicker undergrowth. There they collapsed exhausted onto the soft woodland floor.

Within seconds they had company. The five pairs of eyes anxiously watching the chase from the safety of the woodland also belonged to Moorlanders. Their owners emerged from the trees to the side and greeted their friends joyfully. Rollo remained prostrate on the ground, still winded by the effort of the flight. His two slimmer and fitter companions leapt to their feet, and, Moorlanders being very expressive creatures, hugging and kissing abounded. The five were larger than the three, for they were adults – a patrol from the Moorlander village of Buzzard Woods – and were led by Arken, a burly, red-haired captain of the Buzzard Woods Mark. Arken was an expert bowman, and it was his arrow that had flown straight and true to the throat of the black stallion. His joy in the meeting was the greatest, for Caradoc, the young Moorlander he was now embracing, was his son.

There was no time to be wasted, however, for the three sinister horsemen were still abroad and might even now be seeking them out. One of the patrolmen, Hama, made his way back through the undergrowth to the forest edge. The horsemen were still where they had fallen but the two riders had risen and were tending to their injured captain. Feeling secure in the safety of trees and with his friends close at hand, Hama produced a sling from his tunic and sent a rounded pebble spinning in the direction of the three figures. The pebble fell short but immediately the two standing figures turned and gazed straight at the bush where Hama was hidden. He was gripped by a sudden inexplicable terror. From beneath the black crested helmets peered intent monkey-like faces which seemed to see straight through the leafy covering of the woodland edge. The malice of their glance froze Hama to the spot as the two figures rose and bounded rapidly towards him. Hama could not move and would surely have been caught had not Arken, concerned at his friend's disappearance and waiting for him in the undergrowth, disturbed his trance by calling his name. Hama backed away into the undergrowth. Whether the monkey warriors saw his retreat or sensed the loss of their control of his mind was not clear, but they evidently realised that their victim was lost to them. They vented their rage in a series of shrill screams and howls, and then bounded back to their mounts.

Still gripped with fear, Hama retreated into the forest to rejoin his friends. He sank to the ground and for minutes sat shaking, unable to tell the others what he had seen. Arken now decided that even the edge of the forest held perils and led the whole party deep into the woodland. Hama, still shaking, was assisted by two of the other patrolmen and the party started off in the direction of the river Badgerbrook, about four miles or so into the wood.

Nightfall was approaching and Arken wanted to place as much distance as possible between themselves and the woodland edge. Besides, the river flowed straight into the valley of Buzzard Woods, a deep glacial rift where the Moorlanders' village nestled, remote and inaccessible. Although Arken did not fear for the safety of the Moorlanders in Buzzard Valley, he knew that many of his kin, both young and old, wandered far beyond the confines of the valley and the surrounding woodland. Indeed, not all Moorlanders lived in the valley. For many years now, the lands around the Great Wood, of which Buzzard Woods was only a small and insignificant part, had held little danger for the Moorlanders.

Not since the ancient days had the men of the eastern land dwelt upon the moors and the small bands of roving adventurers which occasionally entered upon this part of the moor usually gave the Moorlanders a wide berth. A single Moorlander was no match for an Easterner, of course, but the Moorlander Mark was courageous and well organised, and such men usually found easier victims amongst their own kind. Bears, wolves and worse, which had once roamed the moors in greater numbers, had now dwindled almost to the point of extinction. An encounter with a bear was a major event, giving rise to great excitement amongst the Moorlanders, and although wolves still roamed the Northmoor, no pack had been seen in the Great Wood for years. Thus, many Moorlanders had left the safety of the forest and returned to live on the open moor, and it was to these and any who might be travelling beyond the wood that Arken was eager to get word.

CHAPTER TWO

BADGERBROOK

The group travelled for an hour or so before they first picked up the sound of the river. To those Moorlanders who dwelt in the valley itself, the sound of the river brought joy. The river was the same that flowed through the valley itself, and its sylvan music carried upon it the sounds and scents of home. Arken's patrol had been absent from the valley for many weeks. They had been sent for reasons which they did not understand to the northern borders of the Great Wood. The period of their patrol had ended and at the time of their meeting with Caradoc they had been preparing for their return journey. The excursion of Caradoc and his two friends onto Saddlemoor Down had less legitimate origins, such that Arken intended to speak with his son on the subject once more important matters had been dealt with. Caradoc, Rollo and the third friend, Michaelmas, had been part of a large group of young Moorlanders camped on the banks of the Badgerbrook. The three friends had slipped away together in the night to search for the whortleberries which grew near the edge of the woods. The whortleberry was much sought after by the Moorlander herbalists for its medicinal qualities and the young Moorlanders anticipated some choice gift in return for them, perhaps even whortleberry pie. Having reached the woodland edge and finding not a whortleberry in sight, they had wandered onto the open moor to climb a nearby tor and view the treacherous marshland that lay beyond. It was here that they disturbed their pursuers. Caradoc knew that he and his friends would have some explaining to do.

When the party reached the river they turned southwards and followed the eastern bank into the thicker woodland. Their hearts lightened as they skipped nimbly over the rounded mossy granite boulders littering the riverbanks. For the moment, the events of a few hours ago seemed a thing of the remote past. The older Moorlanders, though, knew that there was much serious talking to be done and some feared that the events of that day would cast a shadow over the life of every Moorlander, but they did not know why.

An hour or so more brought the group to the edge of Buzzard Valley. They were hailed by the Moorlander lookout – one of two at either end of the valley who remained at their posts more out of tradition than necessity – and soon had the benefit of an escort of excited Moorlander children. The high granite banks of the Badgerbrook fell away into a moss-carpeted depression only a few feet above the water level. Here lay the Moorlander village, some thirty or so wattle and daub huts shaped like igloos – domes as the Moorlanders called them – arranged in two columns along the riverbank. Between the columns, the Moorlanders had constructed their moot – also of wattle and daub – but many times larger than the huts, and the site where all Moorlanders young and old met each month to discuss village business and then to indulge in the great Moorlander passion of feasting. Both activities were presided over by the village elder, Ebenezer, and it was for Ebenezer's dome that Arken now made.

The village elder welcomed him warmly. The two were close friends. Arken's patrol had been away for some weeks and Ebenezer had missed their friendly rivalry. Arken enthusiastically accepted his friend's offer of a jug of cool Moorlander ale and then settled down to tell the tale of his patrol's excursion to the north.

He told of the strange quiet and emptiness the patrol had experienced when it first ventured out onto the open moor. It had followed the course of the Badgerbrook onto the moor and over the great waste to the mire, beyond the tors where the rivers began. The mire lay on the great plateau of the Southmoor across which, in years gone by, the men of the East had travelled to their mines in the West. Confident of their ability to ward off any danger, these travellers rarely took steps to cover their tracks and their camp remains were usually to be found littering the moor. Their untidiness was proverbial amongst older Moorlanders. However, the patrol had found very little evidence of recent visits from the East. Indeed, Ebenezer heard, even the animals of the Southmoor seemed to have left the moor for the safety of the woodland. This, they sometimes did in winter but the leaves were growing on the trees and the sun was shining and the moorland hills should have teemed with wildlife.

Ebenezer looked grave. "Even the birds?"

Arken considered. "Well, we saw some birds – crows mainly and the odd raven. But even the eagles seemed to be in hiding."

Arken then told how the patrol had travelled on to Ryder Hill, the highest tor on the Southmoor. From the summit on a clear day, a tall Moorlander could see the sea many miles away to the south. The tors were taller in those days. But it was to the north that the patrol's eyes were strained. Some miles to the north of Ryder Hill lay the ancient trackway across the moor, which divided the Southmoor from the higher tors of the Northmoor – the Moorland Way. The way was used less often than of old but was still a busy thoroughfare.

Arken and his friends had camped on the summit of the hill for three days without catching sight of a single traveller. But, on the third day in the early evening, two tiny specks came into view travelling westwards. Because of the considerable distance, Arken could not be certain but their size suggested they might be Moorlanders. The two figures had travelled a mile or so under the gaze of the patrol when Hama had drawn Arken's attention to a cloud of smoke – or was it dust? – rising some way to the north of the road.

Arken told the elder of his growing concern as the cloud moved rapidly towards the travellers. At first the two figures had not appeared to notice anything was amiss, but at the last moment, when their pursuers were almost upon them, they had abruptly headed off into the undergrowth to the south of the road. Unfortunately, undergrowth on this high ground was sparse – yellow gorse bushes only, no taller than a young Moorlander – and provided no cover for the pursued. The cloud of smoke was now apparent as four man-sized figures on horseback had hesitated, only to alter its direction so as to intercept its fleeing victims. Within seconds the pursuers were on them. Lassos, invisible to the eyes of the patrol, had encircled the helpless figures, flinging them roughly to the ground. Soon they had been hauled back to their feet and, still bound by their lassos, were dragged, staggering and stumbling, in the wake of the horsemen across the Moorland Way and into the wastes of the Northmoor.

Arken described to his friend the horror he had felt as he watched the two tiny figures slowly disappear, to what fate he could not tell. Distance had prevented the exact identification of the captives but Arken was certain they were Moorlanders. He felt as helpless as they because he could do nothing for them.

Ebenezer heard that Arken's patrol had set out immediately on the return journey. He heard of their chance meeting with the young Moorlanders on the woodland edge and of their peril. Arken felt certain that the monkey warriors who had pursued his son and the riders of the Moorland Way were one and the same. Here, Ebenezer gazed intently. "Not necessarily one and the same," he said. "But from the same source, of that I have no doubt." Ebenezer then told Arken why he and his patrol had been sent onto the moor.

"Some months ago," he said, "I met Ambergris the Grey, elder of the Grimspound Moorlanders. He told me of a group of Moorlanders from the Grimspound Mark – three families, in fact – who had left his mark after a dispute with members of the council. They formed a new settlement on a tributary of the sixth river below Hameldown Beacon. Although Ambergris and his fellows had tried to dissuade them, they did not fear for their safety. Some of their group were doughty warriors and one had been their archery champion four years running. At first they had maintained regular contact with the mark. One of their number had visited the mark each week to collect provisions, usually after the traders arrived from the southern estuaries, but after a few weeks – three or four perhaps – the visits had stopped. Ambergris thought nothing at first, believing that as time had passed they were becoming more self-sufficient and that they would make contact again in a few weeks. But they did not return and Ambergris sent a patrol to investigate. The patrol found nothing – well, not nothing exactly. They found domes, of course – quite well advanced, apparently, for the time they had been there, nearly complete, in fact – and most of the things they had taken but no Moorlanders, none at all."

Here Ebenezer paused, as if lost in thought. There

was silence for a few seconds. The sounds of laughter and juvenile merrymaking drifted into Ebenezer's dome. The clinking of pots and the chatter of children announced that an evening feast was imminent.

Arken was gripped with a sudden sense that the safety of the village was threatened. He fingered the short sword at his side; he would fight to the very last to protect his village from this new threat and there were others who would do the same. He was awoken from his reverie by Ebenezer. "My brother Turmeric was with them."

Arken started. He and Turmeric had grown up together. In the days before the different marks had drifted apart, he and Turmeric had become great rivals on the archery range. Their rivalry had grown into firm friendship, and Arken had often travelled the twelve miles or so to the Grimspound Mark to practise archery and drink ale and elderberry wine.

Ebenezer continued, "The Grimspound patrol stayed at the settlement for three days but no one returned."

"Were there signs of a fight?" Arken asked.

"That's the strange thing," said Ambergris. "Nothing at all. It was as if they had just vanished."

"So," said Ebenezer, "we each decided that our marks would send patrols further into the moor, although what we expected to find we had little idea. Ambergris has also sent messengers to the other two marks to do the same. And on the day of the solstice we shall all meet in moot – all the elders and representatives of each mark. It will be a great honour for Buzzard Woods, the Moorlander Council, which has not met for many years, meeting here in our moot. Old Fortinbras of Drizzlecombe will be hopping!"

"Will the Drizzlecombers come?" said Arken doubtfully.

"Oh yes, they will come," Ebenezer replied confidently. "Fortinbras will not want to be left out, and it's too late to bring the council to Drizzlecombe, and we will get to meet Potentilla of Sheepstor – the talk of the marks – and every bit a match for Fortinbras, or so they say. Whether we'll decide anything is another matter. But one thing is certain," went on Ebenezer, "after the council we'll feast."

Arken laughed. "Talking of food," he said, "I think I smell some."

"Forgive me," smiled the elder. "You must be famished. Let's talk later." Ebenezer winked slyly and tapped the ale barrel as he rose. They embraced and Arken stepped out into the night.

CHAPTER THREE

BUZZARD WOODS

By the time Caradoc and his two companions returned to the village, the other members of their party were long since back. Caradoc, Rollo and Michaelmas soon became heroes as the tale of their escape spread around the village, somewhat embellished in the retelling, it must be said. The monkey warriors become fire-breathing demons mounted on dragons, escape only necessitated by adverse numbers. The temptation proved all too much for the local wag Bluffinch, rather a self-important young Moorlander some two or three years older than Caradoc. His real name was Saul but his haughty gait and puffed-out chest – very much like the bold little red-breasted birds so numerous in the woods – had attracted the nickname and it had stuck. Its recipient blamed Caradoc for it and often used his ample powers of irony in revenge. Bluffinch's version of events involving the three young Moorlanders rescuing the mark patrol from a veritable army of demons was soon all around the village, to the great mirth of his companions.

But Caradoc paid them little attention. The sheer joy of being back in the valley after the horrors of the day put all other things from his mind. He walked to the end of the line of huts and on to the river's edge. He gazed into the water. Beyond the valley the sun was setting in a cleft between two tors. Its light illuminated the water, whilst all around remained in half-light. On the night of the summer solstice only a few weeks hence, when the Moorlanders' great feast took place, the sun set exactly between the tors, and before it finally disappeared below the high valley it turned the waters to a brilliant silver and the surrounding banks to the deepest blue. At that moment, all the Moorlanders of the Buzzard Woods, and the visitors from other marks who came to join them, stood in awed silence until the light vanished. Even woodland animals came to witness the miracle. Caradoc felt sure that the power and mystery of the woods which he felt all about him even now could prevail against the monkey warriors, terrible though they might be.

As he stood there lost in his thoughts he heard footsteps behind him. He turned and saw his father. "There's food to be eaten," proclaimed Arken. Caradoc suddenly felt extremely hungry and together they retraced their steps to the centre of the village where a large trestle had been erected outside the moot. Moorlanders love to eat in the open air and do so whenever the weather permits. Virtually the whole village was there – everyone except Bluffinch and his gang, who had ventured into the woods to recreate the heroics of Caradoc and his friends. Occasionally, their whoops could be heard drifting through the trees.

Caradoc greeted Michaelmas and Rollo, who was close to completion of his second helping of Gorbaduc's delicious fish stew. Gorbaduc was by no means the only Moorlander adept at the art of cooking but he was certainly the most skilled chef in the mark and would act as head chef at the solstice feast. A myriad of other familiar and friendly faces beamed in Caradoc's direction. Old Granny Grizabel rose from her seat and waddled towards him. To his indescribable embarrassment, she flung her arms around his neck and kissed him wetly on the side of the head.

"My little friend has been hunting," she cackled.

"Go away, Granny," laughed Caradoc and his laughter rippled around the table.

The meal continued in the same jocular mood. Bluffinch and his gang returned just in time for the whortleberry pie. As dusk faded into evening, the young Moorlanders retired to bed. Bluffinch led a group of elder Moorlander children into the woods to continue their revelries. Even Rollo and Michaelmas went with them. The adult Moorlanders were left in peace to sip more ale and talk adult talk of councils and weddings and feasts.

Caradoc fancied neither revelry nor conversation. He would visit the badgers!

Of all the woodland animals, Moorlanders love badgers best. They love many other animals, of course, especially the hardy ponies which the Moorlanders' ancestors had tamed for riding, centuries before (a Moorlander, even the largest adult, has great difficulty in riding a horse). The woodland and riverside birds are also much loved, as are the moles. But the relationship with the badger is different. Moorlanders cannot communicate with animals, not even badgers, except for a few badgers who had left their sets, ventured into the open world and learnt the common tongue. Moorlander lore told that the ancestors of the Moorlanders could communicate with badgers; some tales even spoke of Moorlanders who could communicate with the fallow deer but no sensible Moorlander believed these old stories. But Moorlanders and badgers understood one another. They had shared experiences, not only as individuals but as races. Wherever Moorlanders dwelt, badgers dwelt also. It had always been so. Moorlanders believed that badgers and Moorlanders had come to dwell in the moorland river valleys together and that when either Moorlander or badger departed, the other must do so also, or disaster would befall them. And Moorlanders believed that badgers believed this also.

The Buzzard Woods badger set lay on the side of a tor rising out of the trees above the Badgerbrook. Caradoc set off into the cool moonlit night towards the set. Arken saw him go and knew his destination. Young Moorlanders of ten or more wandered freely in the woods around the village and Arken was not concerned. Within a minute or so, Caradoc reached the foot of the tor. The set was some halfway up on the western side towards the river. Some sixteen badgers lived there: three brocks, six sows and seven cubs. As he stepped up the well-worn pathway to the set, he left the track intentionally to crush the wild garlic leaves beneath his feet and release their pungent aroma into the air. It reminded him of feast days. In the bright moonlight, the round granite boulders rose above a woodland sea of white garlic flowers like islands.

He arrived at the set and was greeted by Hamilcar. Hamilcar was the second brock of the set – younger than old Hasdrubal by several years – and but for his great respect for the old brock, he would already have taken over the leadership.

No form of speech passed between them. They faced one another for seconds, and then both turned and plunged into the undergrowth. Hamilcar led and Caradoc followed, along the badger trail. Despite the increasing darkness and the thickness of the overhead foliage obscuring the moonlight, badger and Moorlander forged on at speed deeper into the woodland. Badgers are not the swiftest of creatures and Caradoc would not outstrip the brock but in the dense undergrowth, with birch twigs and brambles about their faces, even a brisk stroll seemed hasty. As the foliage overhead thickened and thinned in turn, so the moonlight waxed and waned. In one shaft of light, Caradoc caught the face of a tawny owl gazing down from the branches of a large oak. The sweet perfumes of unseen woodland flowers drifted in and out of their nostrils. Caradoc began to sense a rhythm in the waves of smells and light. Then all of a sudden the runners burst out into open moonlight. They had risen above the treeline near the summit of the tor and Caradoc had not even noticed that they were going up hill. They slowed and in a few strides were at the very top.

Caradoc stopped and surveyed the vista. In the half-light, the surrounding tors faded into the distance like a shadowy school of humpback whales. To the north, the main body of the moor resembled a solid mass of dark cloud. Caradoc's sight drifted nearer at hand. Below him buzzards wheeled and soared over the woodland canopy, their cries like the mewing of cats. His gaze wandered to Withrell Ridge to the west – and he froze. Along the brow of the ridge three figures on horseback were picking their way slowly and deliberately towards the river. Distance and the poor light concealed their features but from their hunched demeanour and the shapes of the cowls about their heads and shoulders Caradoc knew that he had seen these riders before. He stood dumbstruck for a moment. The sound of low growling beside him brought him to his senses. The large brock was pressed flat to the ground, the hairs along his spine bristling and his fangs bared in a snarl of such hostility that momentarily Caradoc feared for his own safety. His anxiety was overtaken by a sudden sense of panic. What if they came upon the village unnoticed and what if there were more of them? He must get back to warn his father and he must do so quickly. He leapt up and made for the trees. The realisation dawned that without his friend to show him the quickest way, the return trip would take far longer – perhaps too long. But he had no need to fear. Without a sound Hamilcar slipped into the undergrowth and Caradoc followed. Within minutes they were back at the set. Caradoc touched his friend gently on the snout; he knew the shortest way from here.

As Caradoc entered the village clearing, Arken and two other members of his patrol approached him. "Father," he shouted breathlessly, "you must…"

"Hush, we know," said Arken. "Don't alarm the others. There are only three of them and we have sent out patrols to watch them. Go to bed." At that moment the rigours of the day caught up with him. He suddenly felt unbearably tired and his father's advice seemed a very good idea. So he took it.

CHAPTER FOUR

MOOT

The very young Moorlanders were busy decorating the village with summer flowers, chosen as much for their fragrance as their beauty. Garlands of roses, lilac and honeysuckle encircled the domes and even the moot itself.

Just before noon, the first visitors began to arrive: an advance party from the Sheepstor Mark – four stout yeomen evidently attracted by the feast rather than the council.

Shortly after their arrival, news reached the village that brought the mounting excitement to fever pitch. Traders carrying artichokes and asparagus for the feast table had overtaken an old man on a grey pony travelling up the river valley in the direction of Buzzard Woods. Rumours spread like marsh fire around the village that this was Findhorn the Mage.

Caradoc and his friends, returning from their foraging, overheard Bluffinch holding forth to a throng of admiring young Moorlanders. "Findhorn the Great is on his way," he proclaimed. "He is coming to the village to seek me out so that together we may sally forth and give battle to the forces that oppose us."

Not wishing to betray his ignorance of the identity of this celebrated personage when Bluffinch apparently knew him so well, Caradoc hurried off to seek out his father for enlightenment. He found Arken with Hama and his brother Dogstooth reconstructing a collapsed trestle.

"Father, a great warrior is coming to help us," he cried.

"Who?" enquired Arken, glancing up from his work.

"Findhorn, Father."

"Findhorn isn't a warrior," smiled Arken. "He's… well, I'm not sure what he is really. The Grimspounders believe he is a great wizard with spells to control the rivers and the crops, even the weather. Some of them even worship him, but I don't know, I've only seen him twice and I have never seen any spells. He is probably just an old hermit."

"Is he a Moorlander?" asked Caradoc, keen to become as knowledgeable on the subject as Bluffinch evidently was.

"No, I don't believe he is a Moorlander. He is a man and a very old one, but he is certainly not as clumsy and stupid as most men. He understands the ways of the Moorlanders – and of the moor."

At this moment Ebenezer passed and overheard the conversation. "So Findhorn is coming to the council? I had sent messages of invitation to him but I am surprised he is coming. He must know something we don't."

By mid-afternoon everyone had arrived except the Grimspounders and Findhorn. The council had been called for 4pm. Just before 3pm, scouts reported that an old man on a pony was approaching the village from the south. The rumours of his coming and of his great deeds of the past had so captured the imagination of the whole village that everyone, children and adults alike, put aside their chores and lined the southern path to the village to greet him. They did not have to wait long before a hunched, white-haired figure came into view on a small grey pony picking its way carefully between the granite boulders along the riverbank. Despite the obvious distance he had travelled, the rider appeared awkward and uncomfortable astride the grey, and looked even more uncomfortable when he noticed the large crowd who had come to meet him. Ebenezer stepped forward. "Welcome, Findhorn," he said. "We are honoured." Findhorn held out his hand grumpily and placed it on top of Ebenezer's in greeting.

Caradoc was extremely disappointed; this was patently not a great warrior. He was not even armed. No self-respecting Moorlander would have been seen dead in his faded brown tunic. And what was more, he had no hair other than the occasional thin white strand emanating from the back of his head and dangling straight downward. Caradoc glanced mischievously in the direction of Bluffinch and basked for a second or so in his obvious discomfort at the shabby appearance of his hero.

When he looked back at Findhorn, it was obvious to him that this was no Moorlander. Although he appeared no larger than a Moorlander, the flat, open, wide-cheeked features of a Moorlander were missing. The nose was long and thinner and the whole face more narrow. And what is more, Moorlanders did not go bald. Caradoc knew that this was a human.

At that moment, the attention of the Moorlanders was drawn to the other side of the village. The Grimspounders had arrived. Caradoc ran with Rollo and a cohort of excited children to greet them. At the head of the Grimspounders rode Ambergris the Grey, senior elder of all the marks. Ambergris was a marvel. Moorlanders do not generally live past fifty. Ambergris was already fifty-two. Yet despite his ample girth he could ride, joust and drink more like a Moorlander half his age. To the huge admiration of the crowd he rode into the village on a horse – not a large horse, it was true, but a veritable monster compared with the scrawny creature carrying Findhorn.

Caradoc looked beyond Ambergris and his face lit up with joy. Behind the elder, each on a white pony, rode two females. The closer of the two to Ambergris was smiling warmly in Caradoc's direction. She was his mother. Caradoc's mother, Imogen, had lived in the Grimspound Mark for several years. She was a skilled herbalist and healer, and had gone to assist the Grimspounders when their healer had drowned in the fifth river. Caradoc had stayed regularly with the Grimspounders and knew many of them well. He and his mother embraced and she introduced him to her friend, a smiling, elegant lady named Hyperica. He knew her name, she was a renowned archer. But there was little time for pleasantries, as the Grimspounders had arrived late and the council was soon to commence. There would be time enough for mother and son once the talking had ended.

Caradoc took his seat at the back of the moot hall. He could not participate in the discussions, of course, but like the rest of the village, he did not wish to miss a word. The senior elder, Ambergris, opened the meeting. He told of the disappearance of the Hameldown settlers. Other Moorlanders too had disappeared, generally whilst travelling on the open moor. Sometimes there had been evidence of a struggle but often there was an inexplicable lack of any resistance at all. Potentilla, elder of Sheepstor Mark, a wise and un-Moorlander-like presence and the first female to be elected as an elder of a moorland mark, told a similar tale. Her patrol had reported that the monkey warriors had been seen there too, scouring the moor in groups of three or four. Any Moorlanders on the open moor were at risk. Some, like Caradoc and his friends, had been lucky but at Sheepstor two members of the patrol had been killed when a marauding gang had ventured into their coombe and attempted to storm the village. They had been few in number and had been repulsed, perhaps even with one casualty. But the Drizzlecombers reported that they were grim fighters wielding immense spiked maces. They had fallen upon the village in a frenzy, mowing down the lookouts as they came. Their aspect was terrifying but what was more disturbing still was their total disregard for their opponents' great numerical superiority. A foe who does not care for his own preservation, Potentilla had said, is a doughty foe indeed. It was only after the Sheepstor archers had rapidly mobilised and showered them with arrows that they fell back. The following day, two of the villagers digging peat on the moor had not returned.

"Every mark has suffered," said Ambergris. "The purpose of this moot is to consider where our friends have been taken and why, and to decide what steps we should take to bring them back."

Ebenezer then spoke. "That is why I sent messages to Findhorn to attend our council. He knows the ways of creatures who dwell beyond the moor. He can tell us if my fears are correct."

"Let him speak then," said Potentilla.

All eyes then turned to Findhorn. The old man rose shakily to his feet. There followed an uncomfortable silence. The expectant audience began to wonder whether this old dotard could really tell them anything they did not already know. Then he said quietly, "A hundred years ago, many men lived upon the moor. You know this to be true because their ruined dwellings are all around you. The men who dwelt here were of two kinds. My people had inhabited the moor for centuries and first built the great villages. We were a pastoral people. We came to love the moor and its creatures. We built our tombs and religious places on the moor and some amongst us learned its secrets. My father was one of these. We lived in the village of Merrivale, the largest on the moor, and he was our mage. I was the second of four children and our father would impart his art to whichever of us was prepared to listen. He taught us the language of the animals and their ways, the powers of plants – which to cherish and which to shun. We learned to uncover the secrets hidden in the earth and to understand the mysteries of the seasons. He became famed amongst the men of the moor and also those beyond it, and each year on this day, the day of the solstice, men flocked to our village to witness the summer rituals and to share in his wisdom. It was a great village then. Now it is all in ruins."

The old man's speech faltered and he seemed to stare distractedly ahead of him as if lost in his reminiscences. The listeners showed signs of restlessness, obviously doubting what relevance these old tales might have to their present problems.

"But then other men came," Findhorn continued loudly and resolutely as if realising the need to regain their attention. "Men from the East, crossing the moor to reach their mines in the West. Men intent only on destroying. Men whose purpose was to rip from the earth all that they needed, so denying the earth's bounty forever to those that came after them. For a while my people lived peacefully alongside the newcomers but within a few years minor quarrels between us grew into open warfare. Bloody battles were fought all across the moor. We were victorious at Grimspound. They ambushed and slaughtered us in the gorge of the fourth river. But no one could win. The war raged for years and the tors ran with blood, until they sought help. One spring evening, our lookouts on Haytor espied a company eight strong leaving the moor, riding eastwards. Three weeks later they returned, their numbers increased by one, a hunched brown-cloaked and hooded figure, the lookout reported.

"We thought little of it at the time but we came to curse the day that twisted creature first stalked the moor. They had brought him from the Black Mountains in the land to the north of the narrow sea. All that land he had subjugated. There he was known as Magog but our enemies on the moor simply called him the Sorcerer. Whether he was a man or a member of some elder forgotten race like the slaves he later summoned from his mountain fortress, we did not know but he had mastered all the black arts of necromancy and destruction. His purpose in coming here was also beyond our knowledge, but it was rumoured that in return for his assistance against us he was promised free access to the mines of our enemies. Deep beneath the moor lay the means of furthering his black arts.

"His first act was to build himself a stronghold. He chose a site on the high moors to the south of the great tors – a sad bleak place. He called to him his Simians, strange ape-like beings – huge and malevolent, not originally evil but corrupted and nurtured in his mountain home and utterly devoted to him. His castle was constructed in weeks. His next step horrified us and those amongst us who retained contacts with the other side reported that even they began to entertain doubts. He sent out his Simians to destroy each and every living creature on the high plateau of the Northmoor. They butchered the animals and shot down the birds with their crossbows. Woodland is scarce on the high plateau but even the trees were destroyed with diabolical concoctions, mixed in the bowels of the

Sorcerer's castle, which ignited on contact with timber. He loathed all other forms of life and creatures he could not exploit he could not suffer to exist.

"Then he turned his malice on us. The armies of our enemies renewed their onslaughts on our villages but now reinforced by the Simian warriors and armed with the Sorcerer's devilish weaponry. And at the head of their armies rode the Sorcerer himself in a chariot hauled by five huge black dogs. It was rumoured that these were once the dogs of the great warrior Bowerman, stolen by the Sorcerer and perverted to his evil purpose. The savagery of his creatures was fuelled by their terror of the Sorcerer and everywhere our armies were overcome. Our villages were destroyed, our people slaughtered and we were driven from the moor which had been our home for centuries.

"Some amongst us stayed on, hiding in the valleys and the thickest woodland. From these remote places we carried on the fight. But our numbers dwindled. Many more of our people were captured or killed. Those who were taken were not seen again and the rumours of their torments in Magog's dungeons appalled us. So we gave up the battle and retreated even further into the woods and watched and waited. We soon saw that our enemies had been defeated just as we had. One by one their leaders were disposed of. Some merely vanished whilst others died suddenly and without apparent cause. The Sorcerer delved deep and found the riches he sought, and his power became unassailable. Those who had brought him had become as much his slaves as our captive friends. Some of them even escaped into the woodlands and joined our rebel bands and for a while we fought on, but armed with even more terrifying weaponry – iron swords and maces, hogweed whips which blistered the skin horribly on the slightest contact, arrows tipped with the foulest poisons and flaming devices catapulting liquid fire. The Simians now invaded our woodland fortresses, driving ahead of them hordes of terrified Easterners who knew they must either kill us or be cut down from behind. We knew we must either flee the moor or die and sadly we chose the former. One night, after days of heavy fighting on the borders of our valley, we slipped quietly away to the south and left the moor forever. Our people travelled southwards then westwards towards the great river. They crossed it and went away to the west. They set up home on the western moor where they and their descendants still live." Findhorn hesitated again. "The irony is," he said, "that many of the Easterners went with them and more have followed. But I did not go, I fled the moor with them, of course, but did not turn westwards. My home was the moor, my family were there, probably all dead, but I could not contemplate life elsewhere. So I journeyed southward along the valley of the second river until I felt I was beyond the Sorcerer's reach.

"Deep in the limestone gorge I found a cave utterly concealed by the great sycamores and hazels that rose from the valley floor and there I made my home. It was a dark, misty place but I was safe and it has been my home for fifty years. Occasionally, I was visited by fugitive Easterners fleeing from the moor. Most were pale

31

emaciated creatures, their bodies broken after years of slave labour in the mines of Magog. I would do what I could for them but usually their minds were broken also, and after a few days of my hospitality most would wander off into the woodland babbling and deranged, to what end I could not tell. But I had used my solitude well and cultivated the arts I had learned from my father. My valley was lush and free, and there was little I needed that did not grow there. Those who remained with me could help but in most, the memory of the Sorcerer and his Simians was too strong and they stayed only long enough to regain their strength. I began to despair.

"Then one evening, in the depths of winter, an old woman came staggering along the valley. Cold and hunger had almost done for her but I took her in and cared for her, and very soon she revived. Over a meal of mussels collected from the estuary to the south of my cave she told me a tale that warmed my heart. The Sorcerer had taken apprentices in the black arts, young men who were first schooled in utter devotion to their master. Not until their devotion was beyond question did their instruction commence. One student proved more adept than his fellows. Whether through hatred of his master or through mere lust for power, the old lady could not say but the star pupil had proved treacherous. Despite the battery of tasters attending his every mouthful, the Sorcerer had taken poison administered by his student. Too late he had sensed the creeping death coursing through his veins, the spores of the white angel fungus which grows in the deep woods in autumn. Men have no cure for it, neither

I believe do the Moorlanders. He fell into a trance from which he did not wake and the student took his body.

"At first, his slaves could not believe he was gone but a day passed and he was not seen. At the rising of the sun on the second day without him they began to believe the impossible and the tors of the Northmoor resounded with their rejoicing. They planned a feast of celebration that evening to be held in mockery of him before his throne in the great hall of the castle. The Simians, lacking all purpose without his driving will, took no steps to stop them. But at the height of their revelry their joy was transformed to the blackest despair. The great oak door behind the Sorcerer's throne creaked slowly open to reveal a familiar silhouette. The figure approached the throne and then turned to face the throng. The features were the same yet strangely different: the same pale lifeless eyes, the same expressionless gaze and yet somehow less maniacal, more dispassionate and younger. The crowd confronted him, racked with doubt and fearing some deadly blow. Most amongst them no doubt believed this was the Sorcerer recovered from his ordeal and somehow rejuvenated. But some recognised in the sinister figure before them the features of the star pupil transformed by some diabolical process known only to himself into the likeness of the Sorcerer and garbed in the Sorcerer's robes.

"The Simians were under no such doubts. This was evil personified and they flocked to the throne and knelt before him. He milked their adulation for a moment but, soon satiated, he raised an arm and gesticulated imperiously towards the crowd. Instantaneously his disciples turned, charged upon the defenceless mass and proceeded to butcher them with their sabres. Less than a handful escaped to tell the tale.

"The slaughter did not stop at the doors of the hall. Perhaps wishing to impress upon his subjects that he was every bit the equal of his predecessor in cruelty and wickedness, the new Lord of the Northmoor sent forth his Simians to destroy all living creatures he could not enslave. All able-bodied men were seized and imprisoned in the castle dungeons. The women and children were slain. All animals unfortunate enough to encounter the marauders met the same fate. The rest slipped away into the night and made their way into the depths of the woodlands where often they joined forces with the small bands of our people who were still lingering on. In their woodland fortresses, hideous stories reached them of the fate of their fellows in the subterranean mines of the Northmoor. Forced to labour until they dropped in volcanic heat under the eye of the Simian guards, few survived more than a few months. When numbers fell, the Simians took their stallions and scoured the moors for helpless victims to replenish their numbers. Even the odd Moorlander fell into their clutches. But in those days there were more than enough men to extract from the deep the riches which their master craved and his mind did not dwell upon Moorlanders."

Findhorn had spoken for an hour. His audience, restless at first, had soon become enraptured. Even the increasingly pervasive sounds and smells of cooking failed to distract the listeners. Ebenezer felt, however, that this

34

was the time to interrupt. The audience, he feared, might become too alarmed to participate in the coming festivities and the miracle of the solstice would soon be upon them.

"We have all heard of the evil Wizard Lord of the Northmoor but he left the moor years ago and his vile servants with him. Are you saying that he has come again?" asked Ebenezer.

Findhorn appeared surprised at the interruption and even more surprised that the question came from Ebenezer. He hesitated for a few seconds before replying. "I think you know the answer to that. He did indeed leave the moor. He led his Simians back to the mountain kingdom of Magog and re-established his teacher's tyrannous rule over its people. The moor had become too small for him, it was said. But now it seems he is returned. We cannot be sure why. Perhaps the minerals he took from his mines are exhausted and he has come back for more."

Ebenezer nodded in agreement. "That must be true. The settlers from your mark, Ambergris, were abducted, they were not killed – or at least if they were, their bodies were not left. And all the reports we have heard speak of Moorlanders kidnapped and taken away northwards by the Simians. Who knows what torments they are suffering in the heat of those accursed mines." Arken shuddered at the thought of his old friend Turmeric working far underground in the indescribable heat of the northern mines under the merciless eye of the Simians.

Potentilla echoed the thoughts of many. "But who is this usurper? We cannot decide what course to take unless we know who or what it is we face. Does he not have a name?"

All eyes turned to Findhorn for an answer. "The Easterners called him Dewer, a name they use for all those they see as a threat to themselves. You Moorlanders have the name Wistman, I believe. The lore of my people does not tell," answered Findhorn. "Nor does it ascribe to him a past. But if we do not know who we face, we certainly know what we face: a tyrant as deeply versed in the evil arts as his teacher and more dangerous in that he lacks Magog's irrational vindictiveness. The stories which reach us from his mountain kingdom tell of his efficiency and ruthlessness in suppressing all opponents. If, as I fear, he may wish to create a second realm here, then we are in dire danger indeed."

"So," continued Ebenezer, "what this moot must decide is, do we sit tight and wait for him to move against us or do we act ourselves and seek to rescue our friends from his dungeons, a hopeless task though it may seem?"

The starkness of the choice facing them stunned the assembly into an uncharacteristic silence. Nobody really wished to adopt either course and most were now impatient for the moot to end so that the eating could begin. But a decision had to be made.

CHAPTER FIVE

SOLSTICE

Those Moorlanders who had not attended the moot had busied themselves with the hectic preparations for the feast and the subsequent ritual. Giant cauldrons of delicious stew bubbled all along the riverbank. The aroma of herbs and garlic wafted in the direction of the moot and the carcasses of two huge boar, slain by the mark huntsmen, roasted on great spits, providing constant distraction to the hungry delegates.

The time appointed for the feasting to commence came and went, and still the moot continued. Moorlanders, although not known for their punctuality, are rarely late for meals and the delays could only mean that decisions of great importance were being taken. Just after sundown and over an hour after it was scheduled to end, the meeting finally broke up. The four elders had decided to delay the announcement of the moot's decision until the end of the evening for fear of spoiling the celebrations. Whatever harsh decisions had been reached, the Moorlanders pouring out of the moot were obviously putting a brave face on things. Hungry bodies became inextricably entangled in their haste to gain their appointed places on the wooden trestles arranged along the riverbank. After no little effort on the part of the feast stewards, all were at last seated and Ebenezer, as host, rose to address the throng.

"My friends," he began, "I realise that if I detain you long, the food intended for your stomachs may instead find itself travelling in my direction." This comment was met with some laughter but it was plain from the impatient looks on many faces that the time available before food began to fly might be very short indeed. "But if I may be allowed to keep you from your well-earned sustenance for just a few moments longer, in order to welcome our guest. Many of you younger Moorlanders will not have met our guest before but all I believe will have heard the name of Findhorn. Amongst the men of the East, he is accounted a great wizard, a worker of magic. We Moorlanders, understanding more of the ways of nature, know that his skills have been learned from long studies of the earth and its creatures, and call him Mage. Never before have we Moorlanders invited an outsider to attend our summer feast and witness the mysteries of the solstice. But dangerous times are approaching, and men and Moorlanders may well share much more together than feasts. And as for magic, may we find it in the fingers of our cooks."

This latter comment led to rapturous applause which, immediately it subsided, was followed by a universal assault on the bowls of stew which had now appeared before each diner. Whether or not Ebenezer had actually finished, he was certainly not going to be given the opportunity to say any more.

After the first few mouthfuls had been bolted down and the more extreme pangs of hunger satiated, there arose a general hubbub of genial conversation and laughter. Caradoc sat next to his mother. There was much for them to talk about.

Arken, famished after the hours of talk, finished his meal quickly and then leant back and beamed contentedly around him. The glow of happy faces matched the ruddy hue of the sun setting over the western tors. It was not far from the hour of the miracle.

Beside Arken sat Fortinbras, elder of the Drizzlecombe Mark and second only to Ambergris in venerability. A grizzled veteran of campaigns of an earlier age, Fortinbras was reputed to be ill-tempered and surly. He had remained uncharacteristically silent throughout the moot, no doubt still smarting from Ebenezer's success at bringing the council to Buzzard Woods. Moorlander legend had it that the Drizzlecombe Mark was the first to be founded on the moor, and it therefore considered itself pre-eminent and the appropriate venue for all important events. Arken recognised that he would need to tread carefully if he was to engage the old sourpuss in conversation without offending him.

"So, what does our most honoured guest think of

our humble fare?" he opened and immediately regretted that his choice of words might appear sarcastic. Out of the corner of his eye he noticed Potentilla, who, rumour had it, was not averse to the odd witticism at Fortinbras' expense, smiling ironically in his direction. She had been diplomatically seated on the opposite side of the trestle. Fortinbras was plainly not the most honoured guest and the fare was certainly not humble. To Arken's surprise, however, Fortinbras appeared pleased at the tone of the address.

"Ah, Arken," he replied, his rich booming voice stopping several other nearby conversations. "Very fine, very fine, but no more than I should have expected from your Gorbaduc. The finest cook on the moor, it is said. Let us hope that your mark fights as well as it cooks." Fortinbras chuckled loudly, evidently enjoying his own humour.

"You will not find us wanting in that department, if it should come to that."

"I am sure, I am sure," boomed Fortinbras. "But do you have a warrior the equal to our Brand? I doubt that." Fortinbras gesticulated in the direction of a large bull-necked, bristle-headed fellow seated on the adjoining trestle. Arken could see he was falling into Fortinbras' trap. The old windbag had few interests other than the arts of combat and war, and his keenness for arranging mock battles and trials of strength between warriors of the different marks was well known. He tended to attract to him similarly minded individuals. The pugilism of Fortinbras and his companions might well come in extremely handy if dark days were indeed ahead. However, trials of strength could go either way and Arken had heard that Fortinbras was a very bad loser. The last thing that was needed was bad feeling between the marks. Arken, therefore, diplomatically replied that he doubted it too. As well as potentially rather dangerous, Arken also found the course of the conversation was becoming rather tedious. The beauty of the evening and the splendour of the setting deserved gentler banter, and Arken cast about in his mind for the best means of achieving this without offending his guests. Just as he had reached the decision that the only solution was to talk to someone else, he was fortunately relieved of the problem by Ebenezer who again rose to his feet.

"Fellow guests," he announced, "the time is nearing when it is the custom of our mark to congregate on Badger Island to witness the miracle of the equinox but Badger Island is small and tonight we are many. Each mark must select five to go and those left behind may watch from the banks."

Moorlanders are democratic by nature and each mark hastily arranged a lottery to select their representatives. Caradoc was not successful but his father who was, but had witnessed the miracle many times, gave up his place in his son's favour. Some of those selected rowed out to the island but the water was not deep and the distance only a few yards, and Caradoc and some of his young friends waded across.

By the time the last of his party had reached the island the sun had already passed below the peak of the eastern tor. Its circumference a clear, pallid yellow at first appeared to dissolve in a pool of reddening light as it descended gradually and imperceptibly into the hollow between the tors. Caradoc, standing at the fore of the expectant group with his friend Piebald, sensed the rising excitement of the older Moorlanders. Perfect silence reigned both on the island and on the riverbank. From amongst the trees, the woodland creatures gazed out upon the assembly and uttered not a sound.

His attention distracted by the panorama of intent faces surrounding him, Caradoc was looking away at the moment the sun finally nestled into the valley bottom. But he heard the universal intake of breath and saw the valley sides turn a shade of the deepest purple. He turned to face the spectacle. The cleft between the hills seemed filled with liquid of the deepest crimson and from out of this liquid poured their beloved river, its waters a shimmering silver, flowing straight to Caradoc's island, bathing it in light. The young Moorlander stood transfixed but the effect lasted only a moment. A clear, fresh breeze blew off the moor and, as if dispersed by the gust, the light vanished, plunging the valley into a darkness which seemed much deeper than that prevailing a moment before. For a few seconds there was silence. Caradoc was gripped with a sense of emptiness as if something of inestimable value had been irretrievably lost. Arken later told him that he too had once experienced something similar after the solstice, at a similar age, but in later years he had come to recognise the spectacle as a glimpse into the nature of things. Its beauty stayed with them, although not all could see it.

Some time elapsed before the little island had emptied. The Moorlanders drifted back to the banks of the Badgerbrook in small groups and some stragglers remained long on the island, still stunned by the vision. The majority, back in the village, soon recovered their spirits, and the clear moonlit night rang once again with the sound of laughter and revelry but Ebenezer, again the killjoy, soon called them to order.

"Fellow Moorlanders," he called loudly, "I apologise that I must call your festivities to a close but the hour is getting late and you still do not know the decision of the moot." Everyone resumed their seats at the table, save for those few still on the island and Ebenezer continued.

"Hard times are approaching – dangerous times. Times when all the marks must work with one another and with all other creatures who love the moor. We have not always helped each other. Petty squabbles have divided the marks and some have placed their own pride before the common good."

Arken felt that Ebenezer glanced at Fortinbras as he said this but Fortinbras didn't appear to notice.

"But if we make the same mistake now then disaster may befall us." Ebenezer spoke these last words imperiously. Indeed, his voice thundered around the coombe and those Moorlanders still grumbling over the enforced cessation of festivities fell silent. All present felt increasingly apprehensive. What horrors were they about to hear?

"A great evil has returned to the moor," said Ebenezer, his voice sunk almost to a whisper. "An evil which once held the moor in thrall. The Lord of the Northmoor, whose vile deeds are recorded in the mythology of Moorlanders, has come back to persecute us. Already it seems he has enslaved many of our people. He has stolen them away to his mines beneath the Hangingstone Rock and what torments he has subjected them to there we cannot guess. Why he has returned we do not know. What is certain is that while he remains on the moor, our friends will never be free and no creature on the moor will be safe. But what is to be done? That is the question. Your council, to whom the task is appointed to resolve such matters, has asked itself: should we retire into the woods, never venturing forth onto the high moors and hope that he does not notice us? Or, should we unite, seek out all others who would join with us and march against him?"

Ebenezer looked up and surveyed the rows of faces staring back at him. He wondered which alternative they would have chosen. Perhaps they would have preferred a third, not considered by the council.

"Your moot has decided that our wooded valleys will not protect us for long. Eventually, he will come to us. Therefore we must go to him first, before he becomes too powerful and before our friends have died in his slave pits."

Ebenezer knew from the murmur of appreciation that greeted this announcement that the rest of the mark approved the decision. "In three days' time," he continued, "a company of Moorlanders made up of representatives from all four marks will set out eastward. Its quest will be to find the great warrior, Bowerman. Many years have passed since he led the resistance to the armies of Magog, but our friend Findhorn has told your council of a chance meeting with him while wandering in the eastern marshes only a few years ago. He was returning from foreign wars in the land of Karnac beyond the Southern Ocean and those returning with him were full of tales of his valour and prowess. Pray to the Goddess that he still dwells in his old home on the fifth river."

"We must hope beyond hope that he will consent to help us," interjected Potentilla. "He seeks remuneration for his services and he asks much, perhaps more than we can afford."

"And there are others who may offer their help along the way," continued Ebenezer quickly, feeling slightly irritated with Potentilla for appearing unnecessarily despondent.

"The council will await their return at Drizzlecombe, and there we will meet again to consider the report of the company and draw up our plans for the rescue of our friends."

Ebenezer fell silent, his announcement complete, and for a moment it seemed that his words had left his listeners lost in reverie. Much frivolity had been planned for the remainder of the evening and Ebenezer feared that the timing of his announcement had destroyed all possibility of that. Fortinbras, of all people, rescued the situation.

"Come, come, my friends, let's not allow a little wizard from some dull northern land to spoil our fun. Let him dig his holes in the ground. If he digs 'em deep enough, I'll take my trusty axe and knock him into one."

A titter ran around the crowd, the product more of courtesy than of genuine mirth, but the ice had been broken, and slowly but surely the spirit of the night was rekindled and the little valley rang with the laughter of summer.

CHAPTER SIX

THE JOURNEY

The next two days saw frantic preparations for the departure of the company. On the second day it was announced that Fortinbras would lead the company, with Arken as his lieutenant.

That evening Caradoc and his father sat before their dome in the fading light. The warm air was thick with gnats hanging motionless in the pools of sunlight. Caradoc waved vigorously in a hopeless attempt to disperse them.

"But why can't I go if Bluffinch can?" Caradoc complained. "Bluffinch went with the Blackdown Patrol last year. Why is he going again? It isn't fair."

"Bluffinch is older than you," retorted Arken, "and anyway, he has been picked as a reward for his success in the tournament."

"I would have won if I'd entered," Caradoc replied, looking aggrieved, "but I went to see Mother with you."

"And would you rather have entered the tournament than visit your mother?" snapped Arken, now becoming quite irritated at his son's persistence.

Before Caradoc could reply, the unmistakable bellow of Fortinbras boomed out towards them. "Arken, my friend… and young Caradoc. A fine evening but rain is on its way from the sea, I'm told."

Without waiting for an invitation Fortinbras sat down heavily on the end of the same trestle as Caradoc. Caradoc braced himself, expecting the downward force on Fortinbras' end of the trestle to be matched with an equally vigorous upward force on his own. Fortunately, and characteristically, however, Fortinbras seemed entirely unaffected by the laws of physics and, but for a slight jolt, Caradoc remained safely seated.

"We must complete our plans. A successful expedition requires expert planning," announced Fortinbras in a tone that brooked no contradiction.

It suddenly occurred to Caradoc that it might prove considerably easier to persuade Fortinbras to allow him to join the patrol than to convince his father – and now was his chance.

"Did you go on many patrols when you were young, Lord Fortinbras?" he enquired innocently.

"Certainly, my lad," replied the elder, good-naturedly, "and so should all who would one day act as defender of their mark. Why, by the time I was your age I had ridden with more patrols than I can remember and knew the moor better than you modern chaps do today."

Arken saw the way the conversation was going. Either his son would engineer an invitation to accompany the patrol or they would be subjected to a tedious tale of Fortinbras' juvenile heroics. He could not decide which was less desirable and cast around desperately for some means of changing the conversation.

Before he could think of anything, the damage was done.

"You will learn much from me on the coming journey," Fortinbras continued immodestly, "much that you could not learn elsewhere."

This was too much for Arken. "No doubt he would, were he to be travelling with us, but Ebenezer has already limited the number of youngsters to one for fear that the enterprise could be put in jeopardy by too many young ones to look after."

"Nonsense," thundered Fortinbras. "Ebenezer takes caution too far. The young must learn and they can only do so in the field. I am leading this expedition and I say he can come. I will take personal charge of his welfare."

Before his father had the opportunity to take up the argument, Caradoc leapt to his feet, thanked the elder warmly, announced that he must run off and tell his friends the good news and was gone.

Arken cursed the meddling elder under his breath but resolved to accept the inevitable. He had to acknowledge that he did see some sense in Fortinbras' argument. He would spend the next few months in the constant company of the old warhorse and he must therefore make some attempt to get along with him. He unfolded the moorland map brought to the moot by Findhorn, spread it before Fortinbras and settled down to the task ahead.

Caradoc skipped off excitedly and, having reported his success to Rollo and Michaelmas, made off into the woods in search of his friend Hamilcar. It was still only mid-evening, and although the rain clouds that Fortinbras had spoken of were banking huge and purple over the hills to the south, the valley itself was laden with summer sunlight. The young Moorlander jogged merrily along the familiar pathway leading to the badger set. He had nearly reached the final bend when he stopped abruptly and stepped into the dense elder bushes that lined the track. He crouched for a moment, motionless, and then he heard it again: a strangely eerie whistle which seemed to originate from the clearing at the end of the path, only a few yards ahead. The whistle was answered by another. Caradoc wondered whether the sound might come from some rare kind of bird, although it was lower than any birdsong. He was certain he had not heard it before and yet it was peculiarly familiar.

Few creatures are more silent of movement than Moorlanders but Caradoc realised that even he could not approach the clearing unnoticed if he remained in the undergrowth. If he continued along the path he would certainly be seen. Then he remembered the old badger run lying only a few yards below the pathway. He could not see it through the elder bushes but it could only be a matter of feet away – and it ran right up to the clearing.

Caradoc dropped onto all fours and crawled slowly towards the run. In a few seconds he reached it. He then turned and, still crawling, followed the run in the direction of the clearing. The whistle sounded again – a long, elaborately rhythmic sound. He stopped a foot or so from the run's end and, pressing his body flat to the ground, peered underneath the foliage into the clearing. He was amazed by what he saw.

In the centre of the clearing sat Hasdrubal, the senior brock of the set. His old gnarled body was balanced precariously on its haunches with all four limbs extended forwards as if in the act of making an offering. The snout was stretched skywards and the whole frame appeared to shake expectantly. The shaking reached a crescendo and, simultaneously, the old brock threw back his head even further. Then Caradoc heard again the same complex, fluty whistle which had stopped him in his tracks on the path only a few minutes before.

Caradoc's attention had been focused so intently on the strange antics of the badger that for a moment he was aware of nothing else. Then slowly his gaze wandered away from Hasdrubal and across the glade. There, elven and cross-legged on the grass, sat Findhorn. His russet-coloured cloak was pulled tightly over his head, obscuring his features, but it was plain from his outline that he faced the badger, his back arched and his head straining forward. To Caradoc's astonishment a second whistle, indistinguishable in tone from the first, emanated from the cloaked figure. Within seconds Hasdrubal answered – the same fluty sound but a different tune. Had Caradoc not witnessed the spectacle he would have imagined that he listened to two very large nightingales serenading one another from opposite banks of the second river. The exchange continued. Slowly, Caradoc developed the impression that he was peering in upon a scene which both participants would have preferred he had not witnessed. He became a little apprehensive. He felt certain that he had nothing to fear from Hasdrubal or Findhorn and yet there was plainly much about them he did not know. Perhaps they had other powers which they might unleash upon him if they discovered him snooping. He decided to slip away before he was noticed. He backed away into the undergrowth but before the elder branches had closed over his face, the russet hood was cast back and the green eyes of the Mage stared straight at him.

"And who invited you, my young friend?" The tone of the question spoken firmly but with evident good humour set Caradoc's mind at rest. He rose and stepped with some hesitation into the clearing. As he did so, the old brock snorted indignantly, cantered across the glade and vanished into the badger run on the other side. Findhorn watched him go.

"Come," he said when the two were alone, "they'll be missing us back at the village and you can tell me what you're doing here as we go." The old mage clapped his arm round Caradoc's shoulder and together they set off back along the path that Caradoc had trodden only a few moments previously.

"Well, I'm coming with you on the expedition – Fortinbras said I could – and I ran to tell my friend

Hamilcar. But of course I can't tell him… but I was excited… and thought, well, we could be excited together." Caradoc was becoming increasingly confused. Findhorn had that manner of quiet inquisitiveness which makes you say more than you should – and Caradoc was prone to talk too much anyway. Fortunately, Findhorn rescued him.

"Would you like to be able to talk to your friend?" he asked. The significance of the events in the clearing now began to dawn on him.

"Is it really possible?" asked Caradoc.

"For some people, yes, but there is much to learn. My father taught me when I was young. The badgers know much that we do not. We cannot truly understand the world without sharing their knowledge. Tomorrow as we ride, I shall tell you more."

Findhorn and Caradoc re-entered the village as it was settling down for the night. The little valley twinkled brightly with the larger than usual number of lanterns and Caradoc's heart sank at the realisation that this was a sight he would not see again for some time. But the feeling was short-lived and he slept little that night with anticipation of what the morning might bring.

He awoke early the next day. The foretold rain had arrived and the valley sides were shrouded in a thick grey drizzle which the brightening dawn could not clear. Caradoc enjoyed such mornings. The curtains of rain endowed ordinary objects with a sense of mystery and heightened the morning scents. He imagined the spectral shapes of hills rolling away into the distance and wondered what heroic struggles might rage at that very moment in the valleys beneath. And soon, he thought, he would be amongst them.

As soon as he had eaten he ran off to say farewell to Rollo and Michaelmas. The former he found, as he suspected, still intently breaking his fast on a huge pile of ducks' eggs, the empty shells of which littered the entrance to his parents' home.

"Rollo, you glutton. I'm amazed any birds live in this valley with you around." Rollo looked genuinely offended and peels of laughter from Michaelmas, who had overheard Caradoc's comment as he arrived, did nothing to help.

"You know we only eat as much as the steward allows – and he says there have never been so many ducks on the river," retorted Rollo defensively.

"I know, I know, I was only joking," said Caradoc. "I have come to say goodbye. I am going with the patrol to find Bowerman."

"How far are you going?" asked Michaelmas.

"I'm not sure," replied Caradoc. "I think he used to live by the waterfall on the east of the moor but he may have gone into the West or beyond the southern seas. I don't think we would follow him there. Anyway, we're supposed to be back to meet the council at Drizzlecombe in four weeks."

As Caradoc spoke, a huge, exquisitely coloured peacock butterfly alighted on the very egg that Rollo was about to consume. The creature appeared entirely undisturbed by Rollo's approaching hand, as if safe in the knowledge that here in Buzzard Woods all creatures were safe from wanton destruction. Caradoc had no doubt that he would soon enter regions where such trust would be foolhardy in the extreme. His father interrupted his musings. "Come on, Caradoc. The patrol is ready to leave. We will be mounting in five minutes."

"Alright, I'll just say goodbye to Mother."

He hurriedly embraced his two friends and, having promised them a full account of the whole expedition immediately on his return, ran off to the area of the guest-domes where the visitors from the other marks were staying. The Grimspounders had three large domes to themselves and Caradoc espied his mother, Imogen, sitting with the only other female guest, Hyperica. On her lap lay her cat, Temuchin, her inseparable companion.

Caradoc's father and mother had not lived together since he was very young but unlike most parents who lived apart, they still seemed to talk to each other in a friendly way. Caradoc had passed two months in spring and two in autumn with his mother each year since she had left the Buzzard Woods village. Imogen was a skilled healer and the Grimspounders had been without one, their own healer having been eaten by a bear, the last Moorlander known to have met his end in this way.

As Caradoc approached, Temuchin rose elegantly from his mother's lap, flashed her gorgeous orange eyes and arched her back to meet the inevitable caress. "You lazy creature, Temuchin," Caradoc reproached. "Do you never leave Mother's lap?"

"Hush, dear," his mother replied gently. "You'll hurt her feelings." Caradoc was telling her not to be so silly when he recalled the events in the clearing. *If badgers then why not cats?* he thought and held his tongue.

Imogen's views about Caradoc's plans to accompany the expedition were not dissimilar to his father's. Yet, if he had to go, then perhaps this quest might be less dangerous than others to come. She consoled herself that the party would be sticking to the southern and eastern edge of the moor, where so far the monkey warriors had not been seen.

Caradoc and Imogen said their farewells and planned to meet again at Drizzlecombe. Caradoc then ran off to join his patrol, anxious lest it should already have left. The twenty riders and Bluffinch were already mounted. A glance at Fortinbras' face told him that the patrol waited only for him.

"So you think the patrol has nothing better to do than wait for you, do you?" bellowed Fortinbras.

"No, sorry, Fortinbras," Caradoc gasped breathlessly. "I was saying goodbye to Mother."

Caradoc's pony, Nebuchadnezzar, was saddled and waiting for him by his father's side. He mounted quickly and surveyed the assembled group. His gaze immediately fell on Bluffinch grinning across at him. Beside Bluffinch sat Hama. He noticed too his mother's friend Hyperica on a beautiful long-maned roan and sporting a bow and quiver. She smiled reassuringly at Caradoc as their eyes met. How had she got here so quickly? he wondered. On a wooden cart piled high with weaponry and provisions sat Findhorn, wrapped so snuggly in a red cloak that only the top of his bald head was visible. The cart was drawn by two pure white oxen from the Buzzard Woods herd.

Caradoc's survey of his companions was interrupted by Fortinbras' sharp word of command to move off. "Come on, Neb, boy," Caradoc coaxed gently as the whole group drifted forward. The ascent out of the valley was lined with enthusiastic villagers waving and cheering excitedly. Caradoc allowed a backward glance to linger long after the last face had passed out of view. As the patrol picked its way upward along the wooded pathway, the thatched roofs of the village domes slipped in and out of view through the trees. Caradoc found his initial excitement quickly evaporating into a nostalgic longing for home, which increased as the little village disappeared from view and Caradoc's sense of loss was complete.

The patrol proceeded disconsolately onwards through the pouring rain for some miles. The thickness of the summer woodland made progress slow. The sure-footed ponies made easy work of the mossy, boulder-strewn pathways but the cart was another matter, and on several occasions the heftier members of the group were obliged to dismount and physically lift the cart over the larger obstacles.

Fortinbras planned to cover the four or so miles of woodland between the village and the open moor by dusk and pitch camp on the woodland edge. The frequent stoppages jeopardised the timetable but by mid-afternoon the woods began to wane and some rapid progress was made. An hour later, the patrol reached the woodland edge. Caradoc dismounted and gazed through the mist at the vast grey bulk of Harford Moor rising away to the left. Beyond loomed huge purple clouds which Caradoc, had he not known that this part of the moor did not attain any great height, might have mistaken for tors. Despite the gathering dark he could make out the great grey sheets of rain through which the very substance of the clouds emptied itself into the granite mass of the moor. *At least we will be safe tonight,* he thought, *not even the servants of the wizard would cross through that to reach us.*

Camp was constructed with very little help from Caradoc. The Moorlanders sheltered in groups of four beneath felt-covered umbrellas of rafters, erected upon timber stilts. Caradoc and Arken were billeted with Fortinbras and his personal servant, Narwhal. This was not his real name, of course, but a nickname invented by Bluffinch or some other equally heartless Moorlander wag. The reason for it was plain to see, as plain as the nose on Narwhal's face, in fact. Caradoc thought it most cruel but the intended victim strangely seemed rather pleased with it. Caradoc had already wondered what a Narwhal was and was sure that his companion would not be offended if he asked. Narwhal seemed only too pleased to oblige. The name was not a Moorlander word, he explained, and its origins were somewhat obscure. Narwhal believed he had once seen a depiction of his namesake adorning the side of a broken pot. He had found the pot amongst the debris of a deserted man camp along the Moorland Way and was attracted by the weird, long-snouted fish arranged nose to tail around the circumference. Caradoc shuddered at the description. The long snout of the fish reminded him of the voracious pike which swam the moorland rivers. Many a young Moorlander had felt their jagged jaws.

"But, what is more interesting," went on Narwhal enthusiastically, "is that the pot was not a moorland pot. Our mark lore teacher knew of other similar pots from the villages of the men of the West who dwelt in the valley of the great river and sold their tin to traders from beyond the southern seas. And it was these traders who made the pot…"

Caradoc's interest was beginning to wane. This was the sort of thing his father was interested in. Long noses and savage fish were interesting but not ancient pots. As Narwhal droned on, Caradoc's imagination wandered back to the moor. In his mind's eye, a patrol of monkey warriors mounted on black stallions galloped furiously down off the nearest tor towards the unsuspecting camp. Their leader, Caradoc had seen before, the same sinister figure that had pursued him and his friends over Saddlemoor, and, thwarted on that occasion, he was returning again for his intended victim. His bloodied brow bore the marks of his stallion's hooves, brought down by his father's arrow, and he sought revenge. The thin cries of the riders were drowned out by the torrential rain and they approached the camp undetected.

"Come on, it's past eight." Caradoc woke with a start. His father knelt beside him about to prod him out of his slumbers. It was morning and brilliant sunshine flooded in under the canopy.

CHAPTER SEVEN

BIRDSONG

Caradoc felt immediately guilty that he had apparently fallen asleep while Narwhal was telling his life story. Any apologies would have to wait, however. The tent was beginning to lurch alarmingly and Caradoc feared that it would soon be packed away whilst he was still inside it. He rapidly threw on the first tunic he saw and peered out between the door flaps. All about him was activity. His was the last tent standing and a few feet away from him Narwhal was struggling awkwardly with a guy-rope.

It vaguely crossed Caradoc's mind that Narwhal was collapsing the tent upon him as a retribution for his rudeness but all thought of such mean-mindedness was dissipated by the genial grin which greeted him.

"Morning, old chap," beamed his friend.

"Want a hand?" Caradoc offered, beginning to fear that the tardiness in dismantling his own tent was not due to his continued occupation of it but to the incompetence with which the task was being undertaken.

"No, no... go and have some breakfast," said Narwhal and merrily waved his arm in the direction of the moor.

The smell of frying food was everywhere in the air and Caradoc's gaze followed the direction of Narwhal's arm to where four or five other late risers were congregated around a roaring fire, consuming a breakfast of fried bacon, mushrooms and parsnips. Caradoc hurried off to join them.

His fast soon broken, he returned to give Narwhal some badly needed assistance. As he was doing so he noticed his father, who had disappeared immediately after awakening him, striding in the direction of the camp in the wake of Fortinbras.

"Come on, come on, we don't have all day," grumbled the elder impatiently. "We've miles to go."

"Where are we going?" Caradoc asked his father as he hurriedly prepared his pony for whatever journey lay ahead.

"We're going south."

"South? Why south? I thought Bowerman lived on the moor."

"We aren't really certain where he lives. Last night Findhorn, Fortinbras and I met in Findhorn's tent. Findhorn has an ancient map drawn by his people in the days of the wars."

"Oh, can I see it?" Caradoc exclaimed excitedly. He

loved maps, especially old ones, and would pour over them for hours.

"You could have seen it last evening if you hadn't spent all of it sleeping," Arken retorted good-naturedly. "But it hasn't gone anywhere. We'll look at it this evening. Anyway," he went on, "Findhorn's messengers believe that Bowerman no longer lives by the falls on the east of the moor."

"Messengers, what messengers?" Caradoc interrupted again.

"Must you constantly interrupt?" Caradoc sensed that his father's evident impatience derived from the fact that he had as little idea of the identity of these mysterious messengers as he had, but the answers to his questions would have to wait, as a bellow of command from Fortinbras summoned the patrol to mount.

As the patrol moved away across the moor, Caradoc took one last longing look over his shoulder at the disappearing woodland. The great rounded, powerful shapes of the oaks, beech and ash constituted a reassuring security that was entirely lacking on the open moor. A Moorlander would face an enemy in the heart of the ancient woodland safe in the knowledge that this was his realm and that he knew its wiles and its ways. On the open moor he had no such advantages and the element of surprise might favour his enemy. Caradoc nervously scanned the surrounding tors. The heather-strewn slopes were littered with little hillocks of granite boulders, looking as if they had been scattered there at random by a passing giant. What if a patrol of monkey warriors lurked behind each granite pile awaiting the call to swoop? Caradoc concentrated his gaze on the nearest rock pile for some minutes, leaving his trusty Nebuchadnezzar to pick his own way between those, albeit somewhat smaller, lumps of granite lying in their path. But for an angry bird which rose noisily and awkwardly into the air as they passed, the granite seemed to hide no secrets, and his fears subsided as the course of the patrol bent slowly southwards away from the rock-strewn slopes and back towards the thick swathe of woodland encircling the southern foothills of the moor.

After a while Caradoc became aware of Findhorn drawing alongside him. "So, you want to talk to animals?" enquired the old man.

"Is it really possible?" Caradoc replied.

"Many would ridicule you for believing so," said Findhorn, which did not really answer the question.

There was a silence for a moment and Caradoc wondered why Findhorn had raised the issue if this was all he intended to say. The Mage continued: "Many years ago before the Easterners came to the moor, two languages were spoken here. One was the same language which you and I speak today, but another older tongue was known to some – to those, both Moorlanders and men, who cherished memories of an earlier age. Few even then knew all its secrets but those who did spoke of a time when it was known to all the higher creatures – the common tongue, they call it."

"Did such a time really exist?" interrupted Caradoc yet again.

"I doubt it very much," replied the old man to Caradoc's profound disappointment. "Even by my day, most species of animals had forgotten it entirely. I have never met an ungulate who knew a single syllable."

"What on earth's an ungulate?" interrupted Caradoc yet again.

"An animal with hooves," replied Findhorn. Caradoc was impressed by the spontaneity of the reply but then he remembered that his companion was a mage and really should know these things.

"Like pigs and sheep, you mean, but aren't they very stupid anyway?"

"Well, I couldn't really say," replied the old man, "as I have never spoken to any." Caradoc could not really fault the logic of the reply and so resolved to adopt a different line of questioning.

"So which animals could speak?"

"Well, badgers certainly, as you've already heard. It was said that rabbits could – although I have never heard one – and one or two old bears and cats... yes, the moorland cats were very proud of their eloquence in the common tongue but then you know how vain cats are." Caradoc thought of Temuchin and resolved to speak more politely of her in the future.

"There was one cat, the leader of a colony of cats near Sheepstor – the cat of cats, he called himself – who claimed to be the only living creature who knew the entire language."

Caradoc listened, spellbound, and as he did so, the determination to learn the language grew within him.

"Tell me some words," he prompted. "Tell me some words so that I can learn."

Caradoc saw immediately that Findhorn was irritated. "Words? What do you mean, words? There are no words," he snapped.

"But... but how can they speak?" Caradoc stammered. "How can they speak without words?"

"Despite your age, you have the curse of Moorlanders and men. You believe that you are superior and it is beyond your comprehension that other creatures have skills more subtle than your own."

Findhorn seemed to be about to continue in this vein but a glance at his young companion's crestfallen expression was enough to dissuade him. He sensed he had gone too far.

"But I love animals and so do most of my friends."

"I'm sure you do, and Moorlanders aren't as bad as men and I've no doubt you aren't as bad as some Moorlanders," Findhorn conceded. "But you should still not assume that all life operates by your own standards. The common tongue is not constrained by words. It is a language of tone, texture, cadence and melody. You might think it music rather than speech and you hear it every day."

Caradoc was astounded. "When? How?" he blurted.

"In fact you're listening to it now."

Caradoc strained his ears, desperate to hear. The clip-clopping hooves of the patrol's ponies drowned out most other sound. In the distance murmured the waters of the fourth river. The patrol had crossed it only half an hour ago. Almost immediately overhead he heard the frantic twittering of an unseen skylark. Then the realisation dawned.

"Birdsong," he fairly yelled. "You mean birdsong." Other members of the patrol engaged in their own conversations looked around in surprise. Bluffinch, only a few yards in front, almost fell off his mount in alarm.

"So birdsong is part of the common tongue but badgers don't sing like birds."

"Of course they don't but they still sing. The tone may be harsher but the meaning is the same."

Caradoc thought for a moment. "So I can talk to Hamilcar?"

"Not unless you spend many hours learning, and there is only one person who can teach you."

"You, of course," laughed Caradoc, interpreting this as an offer, and as they rode on they drew up their plans for the first lesson.

By mid-afternoon the patrol had completed the descent of the steep escarpment of Ugborough Moor and turned southward along the narrow winding valley of the fifth river. Good progress had been made without mishap, and the Moorlanders looked forward to an early camp and a tasty supper once the wooded banks downstream were reached.

Caradoc's eagerness for campfires and eating drew him slowly to the fore of the group, which by now was straggling out for the best part of half a mile. Bluffinch alone kept up with him but little conversation passed between them. Caradoc contemplated the day when he would be fluent in the common tongue. He wondered whether Bluffinch would bother to learn it.

The circumnavigation of a low egg-shaped hill to the west of the river brought the two riders to the first of the gnarled little trees straddling the rocky riverbank. Caradoc's gaze followed the course of the river southwards to the taller, thicker woodland beyond. That would be where camp would be struck.

He stopped at the first tree and wondered whether to enter. He looked back along the river. The egg-shaped hill obscured the remainder of the company from view. Even the sound of the ponies' hooves and the inevitable chatter of their riders was submerged beneath the rushing of the waters tumbling down off the moor in the riverbed and in a host of tiny rivulets feeding it from every side.

His hesitation afforded Bluffinch the opportunity of entering the wood first.

"Come on then, if you're coming," exclaimed Bluffinch, oozing self-satisfaction. There was nothing for it but to follow and the two riders forged on. The strange twisted trees made Caradoc uneasy, especially as there was still no sign of the rest of the company, but the deeper woodland brought with it the sturdy, familiar trunks which reminded him of home. Caradoc sensed that he was entering woodland at a similar altitude to his own dear Buzzard Woods.

He peered ahead of him to make sure he was not alone. Some twenty yards or so ahead the broad back of his companion rose and fell gently with the roll of his equally broad-backed pony. His gaze was drawn to a rustling in the foliage immediately above his friend's head. A black snout thrust its way through the leaves, followed by a huge brown mass which appeared for a second to hang unsupported in the air. Then the horrible realisation dawned that this was not the body of some strange denizen of the trees as it had first appeared but the head of some even vaster creature, standing like Bluffinch's pony on the ground.

Stupefied, Caradoc watched as the brown mass parted to reveal a cavernous mouth lined with teeth, every one of which seemed as large as the dagger at Caradoc's side. The huge jaws salivated and looked about to engulf Bluffinch's head. He must do something. He half screamed, half spluttered, "Bluffinch, look out!" Most of the sound was lost in his throat but it did the trick. The strangeness of the cry startled Neb, who stumbled, throwing him forward. By the time he had regained his position the huge apparition had vanished, back into the wood from whence it came, and he was confronted only by a slightly alarmed-looking Bluffinch staring back at his redeemer as if he had gone mad.

CHAPTER EIGHT

HYDRAX

"What are you squeaking about?" he enquired, half in amusement and half in irritation. The look of obvious terror on Caradoc's face changed his tune.

"Didn't you see it?" gasped Caradoc.

"See what…? What did you see?"

"It was a…" Caradoc hesitated, unsure where to begin.

To the immense relief of both, the clip-clopping of hooves foretold the arrival of the rest of the company. Hama was the first to reach them. He immediately sensed their disquiet.

"What's wrong, what's happened?" he enquired.

Caradoc realised he had to pull himself together. Whatever he had seen might come back and the company would have to be prepared. But what had he seen? Findhorn would surely know.

By this time, both the old man and his father, who together had been bringing up the rear of the party, had arrived and the whole company dismounted.

"Well, lad, what's afoot?" bellowed Fortinbras in a voice loud enough to summon every dangerous creature in the area.

Caradoc resolved not to attempt to interpret what he had seen but merely describe it as it had happened.

"Well, I was riding along this path. I was just where I am now… and Bluffinch, he was up there ahead of me. I heard a rustling in the bushes and then I saw…" He hesitated, still not absolutely certain that he had really seen it.

"Yes, yes, go on."

"I saw an enormous head. It must have been as high as the treetops."

"Anything else?" snapped Fortinbras, apparently sceptical of the whole affair.

"Well, it had teeth."

"Heads normally do," interjected Bluffinch with feigned levity. No one laughed.

Findhorn had remained silent while Caradoc told his tale but now spoke.

"We must press on," he said. "We must reach a suitable clearing for camp before dark. I do not know these woods. We may still have far to go. We must keep to the centre of the path, away from the trees and each must watch over his fellows."

70

The company remounted in silence. Obviously, Findhorn was taking seriously the tale of this mysterious monster lurking in the forest. In the failing light, the thickness of the undergrowth constituted an impenetrable barrier beyond which the hugest enemy might prowl undetected until it struck. The riders proceeded in single file never more than a few feet from the trees. The hoped-for clearing seemed nothing more than a dream. Each bend in the trail brought disappointment and as the last light began to wane, a sense of panic set in. How would they fend off any attack from an unidentified invisible foe? Then, just as utter blackness enveloped them, a whoop of joy from Hama, who led the column, announced their good fortune: a perfect campsite.

The trail opened out into an enormous clearing, almost as large as the hollow of Buzzard Woods village, and almost in the centre, a large grey mass denoted the outline of a rocky outcrop – an ideal sanctuary for the Moorlander camp beds. And it did indeed seem that their luck had changed, for at that moment, the covering of clouds parted and the light of an almost full moon flooded the clearing.

"Perfect!" exclaimed Findhorn as the vista opened out in front of him. "I couldn't have designed it better myself."

But the welcome moonlight illuminated more than just the clearing. As each pony entered the light, its rider expressed approval and delight at their good fortune. All except the last – for the last pony was riderless.

For a second the company was speechless, blinking with disbelief at the bare back that should have carried their friend Romulus. Fortinbras was the first to react.

"Arken, Hama, Hengist [this was Narwhal's real name, his master did not condescend to nicknames], quick, with me, into the undergrowth. Go in pairs. You and Hama take the riverside," he yelled at Arken. "Hengist, this way with me but don't go too far. Keep within earshot. Hyperica, cover us with your bow."

The others looked on, their emotions torn between terror of the great beast lurking in the darkness and desperation at the plight of their missing friend. A few others looked about to follow Fortinbras back into the woods. They were brought to their senses by Findhorn.

The old man knew well that Fortinbras' excursion was hopeless but he knew equally well that Fortinbras would not take his word for it. He would only hope that all four would come back. He shepherded the remainder of the company towards the granite pile at the centre of the clearing.

"Caradoc, you and your friends collect some brushwood. We need two large fires on either side of the rock. It won't like flames."

Findhorn's instructions were aimed as much to distract the company from the horror of the moment as for any defensive purpose. But even if two hefty bonfires would not dissuade the creature in the woods from attacking, at least they would see it coming. Within seconds the group was all activity, busy figures scurrying here and there in the moonlight. Some piled high the brushwood while others transformed the bare granite rock into a little village. Before long, the task was complete and the company lapsed into nervous inactivity, no one feeling able to embark on the more mundane tasks of unpacking or cooking, while the rescue party remained in peril. They waited in silence save for the roaring and crackling of the fires, every ear straining into the night. An owl wailed eerily from the direction of the river, and a pair of pipistrelles flitted frenetically in and out of the firelight, oblivious to the drama unfolding around them. As the minutes passed, Caradoc felt a mounting sense of panic. Surely they would return – they must!

Several of the older Moorlanders suggested despatching a second group to seek out the first. Findhorn pointed out the folly of consigning any more of their number to blunder blindly in the darkness but the general consensus of opinion was that anything was better than waiting helplessly for what seemed an inevitable outcome. Tempers were becoming frayed, when to the unspeakable delight of the company, the bedraggled figure of Hama burst through the undergrowth, followed closely by Arken. Caradoc screamed with joy at the sight of his father and ran forward to greet him. As he did so he was stopped in his tracks by a succession of events which seemed to happen at once. A low rumble emanated from amongst the foliage on the opposite side of the clearing, rising through a snarl to an enraged cavernous bellow. As if propelled by the sound, Fortinbras and Narwhal hurtled into the clearing, blinking stupidly in the glare of the firelight. The latter bore the lifeless body of the unfortunate Romulus. In their wake, the branches parted and the most enormous creature Caradoc had ever seen stepped into the light. It was a gigantic cave bear – a relic from primeval days – the like of which the moor had not witnessed for many a year. A shower of Moorlander arrows rained upon the beast from the quicksilver bow of Hyperica as it strode into the clearing but it flourished its huge black arms and brushed them aside, perturbed not at all by the few which pierced its flesh. Findhorn appeared before the creature, to what purpose Caradoc could not guess, for surely there was nothing which could prevent the monster from reaching their campsite and wreaking havoc

A spear the size of a young sapling flew through the air from an unknown source and entered the bear's side. A huge paw snapped its shaft but the point had found its mark, and the beast screamed in rage and agony as its futile attempts to dislodge the weapon only succeeded in embedding it deeper. It turned and vanished back into the wood. Caradoc's gaze retraced the flight of the spear. On the edge of the clearing, diametrically opposite the point where the bear had re-entered the wood, a shadowy figure emerged from the undergrowth. But for its gait, smooth and erect, Caradoc might have initially mistaken this for another cave bear. The shadow cast by the firelight exaggerated its size and the flickering silhouette loomed immense against the leafy screen beyond.

A few strides were enough to reveal that this newcomer was certainly no bear. The figure advanced confidently towards the rock to be greeted with obvious relief from Findhorn.

"Bowerman!" he exclaimed in a tone as close to excitement as the old man could muster. "How did you know we were coming?"

"I didn't," replied the newcomer. "I came up the valley to seek out Hydrax the bear. He passed through our woodlands the night before last, leaving wanton destruction in his wake. He did not know of my presence. I fear I have lost him now."

The great warrior did not look too upset at his loss and within seconds was lost in the profound discussion with Findhorn – evidently an old friend. Fortinbras, who considered himself an equal in prowess to the legendary pugilist, looked jealously on, neither introduced to the newcomer nor invited to participate in the deliberations. The elder's reservations were not shared by his fellows who were only too happy to have this formidable new friend on their side.

Whatever private matters Bowerman and Findhorn had to discuss did not detain them long and within a few minutes they had joined the large group gathered around the fire. Caradoc studied the newcomer in more detail. Even seated cross-legged in the circle he seemed a figure larger than life and built on a different scale to any man Caradoc had ever seen. His broad shoulders hovered above the heads of those surrounding him, and his brown hair vest and thick red beard might have been shorn from the hide of the great bear he had just seen off. Piled behind him was the heap of weaponry he had discarded before sitting down: a spear, the twin of that which had repulsed the cave bear, a bow as tall as Bowerman himself and a great broadsword which Caradoc doubted he could lift, let alone wield.

Caradoc's gaze wandered from the instruments of

battle to the face of their master. He started slightly. He was now not so sure whether he was looking at a man. The contours of the lower face were those of a man certainly but above the eyes, heavy protruded brows were set against an even heavier forehead. The features carried about them an air of strange familiarity and for a moment Caradoc felt uneasy, even intimidated by the newcomer.

However, any such feelings quickly vanished as he looked into the eyes below the brows. The eyes were those of a Moorlander, warm and kind, and yet far sadder than the eyes of any Moorlander he had ever seen. Caradoc knew he was not looking at a Moorlander but he also knew he was looking into the face of a friend.

As he stared, Bowerman became aware of his interest and the heavy features became transformed into a broad smile. Caradoc smiled back. The big beaming face before him seemed to grow until it filled his entire consciousness. The image was still with him when he awoke, blinking in the sunlight.

CHAPTER NINE

THE RINGS

The new day was a scorcher. Rising late as always, Caradoc was surprised to find the campsite virtually empty. A few of the older members of the company sat around cleaning their weaponry or preparing breakfast. Findhorn, Fortinbras and his father were huddled in a circle pouring over a map. Bowerman was nowhere to be seen. Caradoc, drawn by the map, was about to become an unwelcome fourth member of the group when he was distracted by a sombre spectacle on the edge of the clearing. The three remaining Moorlanders had constructed a wooden sled of oak saplings bound with twine, to which they had strapped the body of poor Romulus. Two ponies were needed to haul their dead companion to his ultimate resting place and Caradoc volunteered the services of Neb. Narwhal, who was organising the rites, gladly accepted. He explained to Caradoc that the rest of the company had gone on ahead with Bowerman to the latter's home further down the river. There they would bury their fallen comrade, in the barrow of Bowerman's ancestors. He had no family in the Moorlander Mark and it would be an honour for him to lie with such esteemed company and cement the relationship between Bowerman and their people.

Caradoc asked whether anything more had been seen or heard of the bear. Narwhal reassured him that it had not but it was evident from the general haste with which the preparations were conducted that all were keen to move on in case the creature should return. Caradoc grabbed a few remaining morsels of breakfast and, shortly afterwards, the party departed the clearing, each sincerely hoping he would never return.

They made for the river, moving slowly as Caradoc and his father proceeded on foot. The nocturnal terrors of the previous night evaporated in sunshine and birdsong. Blackbird, robin and blackcap seemed hidden behind every leaf, and Caradoc's spirits rose and then fell again with the guilty realisation that he was rejoicing in the company of the body of his dead friend. He thought of other Moorlanders he had known who were no more and of the stone chambers in which they now lay. He remembered the speeches of Ebenezer and the burial rites. Death was sadder for those who remained, he thought – those who would not see their friend again. The dead were merely returning home, to the Mother Goddess, to become part again of all the beauty he saw around him; part of the blackbird singing joyfully just above his head and of the oak tree in which it sat. Thus musing, Caradoc was easily convinced that his feelings of guilt were unjustified and that he was quite at liberty to go off and enjoy himself.

It was still quite early and the waters rising from the riverbed to meet the sunshine formed a white snake of hazy mist, curling off down the valley. The clarity of border between mist and woodland was quite startling and it seemed to the young Moorlander that if he stepped from the woodland he would disappear utterly from sight.

The company turned southward and moved at a leisurely pace down the valley. Findhorn advised that without hurrying they would reach Bowerman's home by mid-afternoon. As they forged southward, the countryside changed slowly but perceptibly. The little gnarled oaks grew into huge broad-leaved and broad-branched leviathans. As the river slowly widened, little islands shrouded in weeping willow and silver birch beckoned to the travellers with hints of unseen treasures concealed beneath the leafy canopies. If the Goddess still dwelt in the world, Caradoc thought it would be here. He extracted from Arken a promise to return in less dangerous times with his father's coracle to explore each and every one.

By noon, the company had entered a steep-sided ravine. The shade afforded by the cliffs and the tall trees came as some relief from the midday sun. As the waters squeezed their way between the rocky banks, the flow was quickened and a hundred little cascades threw up a spray which further refreshed the travellers. Some of the group, Caradoc included, took advantage of the numerous deep pools that interspersed with the areas of rapids for some midday bathing.

Eventually, Findhorn called the party to halt and waved an arm in the direction of the hills.

"There lies the home of Bowerman," exclaimed Findhorn dramatically. "Even the Lord of the Northmoor would not enter there."

Astride the brow of the next hill, the outline of giant earthworks loomed against the sky. The company followed a winding pathway rising up through the tree line to the open fields above. From above the tree canopy the valley bed and the ribbon of blue coursing through it were no more than a guess, wholly obscured by the blanket of billowing green that filled the valley as far as the eye could see. As they progressed, the incline became more gentle, and Caradoc, to the fore as always, could make out great earthen rings beyond which lay a smaller, strangely rounded hill, too perfect to be the work of nature.

A sudden gust of wind carried on it the sound of familiar voices, and Caradoc was about to run forward to greet the advance party when a gruff and wholly unfamiliar voice stopped him in his tracks.

"Who has business with Bowerman the Warrior?" it fairly snarled from behind the outermost ring. He was about to answer that Findhorn the Mage and Fortinbras, Elder of the Moorlands of Grimspound had such business, when the spectacle which presented itself in an opening to the circle rendered him incapable of any response whatsoever. An elongated striped snout, appearing to balance a large black beetle on its tip, thrust itself heavenward. In its wake stumbled noisily forward the broad, bewhiskered frame of an enormous brock. For a moment Caradoc feared the creature was about to attack him. He was reassured by the arrival of his father and Findhorn.

Caradoc stared at the apparition in disbelief. It was not the pugilistic stance that astounded him, nor the bristling weaponry. The creature had spoken to him, not in some strange badger version of birdsong that only Findhorn could understand, but in plain and simple language, intelligible to the most stupid Moorlander.

Findhorn plainly did not share Caradoc's surprise.

"Wolfsbane, what brings you here?"

"Moorlanders bring me here," rasped the reply, "or rather I bring Moorlanders here." The speaker's contempt for Moorlanders was evident in his voice.

"Grimspound Moorlanders captured by monkey men. We fight them by the sixth river. They fall on us from the trees – twenty or thirty. They whoop and scream. They are mad with rage but they cannot overcome us and we slay them in droves. They flee in panic and when they have gone, our companion lies dying. As we tend him we hear the cries of their captives caged in the woodland. We release them from their wicker cages and bring them here with us. They owe us their lives."

This was too much for Fortinbras. "Well, we only have your word for that," he said.

Wolfsbane glared at Fortinbras with a look of such malice that Findhorn quickly stepped between them. "Well, let's go and find them," he coaxed.

The brock grunted dismissively and turned away. He waddled off in the direction of a strangely adorned oval-shaped tent pitched well away from the other dwellings. Before the tent, three other large brocks sat busily tending their weaponry.

The company advanced beyond the second ring within which lay a large flat open sward. The ponies of the advance party grazed peacefully at the southern end and Caradoc recognised some of his friends setting up camp beyond. As he approached the inner circles he realised why the central mound had appeared so strange from afar. It was entirely hollow and Caradoc espied in a dark doorway the tall figure of Bowerman. The mound was the hunter's house and Caradoc could not wait to explore inside it.

He felt Findhorn's hand on his shoulder. "Come with me to the summit of the mound. You can see all the world from there."

Caradoc followed the Mage up a short winding path to the top of the mound and clambered onto a low lookout platform. Findhorn clambered up alongside him and pointed due north back in the direction of the moor. Caradoc's gaze followed the winding path of the river northward through low green hills and even greener woodland. In the middle distance the foothills of the moor rose starkly above the southern lowland, a hazy tapestry of purple heather and yellow gorse, and on the edge of their field of vision stood the higher tors. Findhorn pointed out each one to Caradoc and named them. The twin rocky peaks of Haytor looking as if split in two at the very summit by a giant's axe; beyond, Houndtor, its granite pinnacle appearing on the point of exploding forward and rushing down the side.

"Beyond Houndtor," explained Findhorn, "a mile or so on lie the Becka Falls where Bowerman once dwelt and where Wolfsbane, whom you have just met, now lives."

Findhorn then turned full circle, looking due south. The haze was thicker in the warmer southern air but Findhorn pointed out a dimly visible flat headland virtually at the limit of their field of vision.

"Can you see that high point where the land falls away?"

Caradoc strained into the distance. "It's the sky… no… surely it can't be the sea?"

"That's exactly what it is. You can see the whole world from here."

"But I never realised it was so small. I've never seen the sea before. I've only heard stories about it, dreamt about it. I never knew it was so close."

"Well, it isn't that close," said Findhorn. "As I said, you can see a long way from here."

Findhorn directed Caradoc's attention away to the West. The hills rolled away into the distance, interspersed with ribbons of mist, denoting the courses of numerous little rivers tumbling from the moorland to the sea.

"That way lies my home," said Findhorn quietly. The old man gazed for some minutes westward while Caradoc continued to survey the whole panorama laid out before him.

"Well," exclaimed Findhorn eventually, "we'd better go back down. We have much to discuss this evening."

As they retraced their steps, Caradoc's curiosity about the badger finally boiled over. "Who was that awful creature? He's just like Fortinbras, only worse!"

"Yes, he is insufferable," laughed Findhorn. "And he brags as much as Fortinbras. But there I think the similarity ends. Fortinbras may be a conceited windbag but beneath it all, there is a kind heart. I do not believe there is much kindness in Wolfsbane. Indeed, in many ways I wish he were not here at all."

"Why not?" enquired Caradoc. "Won't he fight with us?"

"He might – if we pay him enough," Findhorn replied. "He and his band are mercenaries. They congregate wherever there is rumour of war. It is said by some that Wolfsbane can sense the advent of war from afar and once he arrives in a place, war is inevitable. His presence confirms my worst fears."

"But isn't Bowerman a mercenary too?"

"Yes, but of a wholly different kind. He is one of the last of a proud and ancient people. Indeed, he may even be the last. Once, his people – the Gigantici – were spread throughout the northern lands. But I have not seen another for years, nor heard of one. Bowerman seeks payment for his services – that is true, he has to live somehow. He is no farmer, no artisan. But, if the cause is good but the victim poor, he will often help without payment and no matter how great the reward, he will never fight for a bad cause.

"Wolfsbane and his crew are different. Their skills are available to the highest bidder. I heard that they changed sides three times in the Armorican wars."

"Might they fight against us?" Caradoc asked, alarmed.

Findhorn thought for a while. "No, I do not think they would. I think Wolfsbane would realise that this is no ordinary foe. If he overcomes and enslaves us he will not stop here. Eventually, there would be no one to enslave and therefore no more wars. Wolfsbane would not wish to live in such a world, nor would he wish to be subjugated to such a tyrant. He will fight with us, though we may well have to pay him."

By now they had rejoined the others in the inner ring where all was activity. Fortinbras was interrogating Grimspounders concerning their ordeal. Everyone else seemed occupied with either weaponry, ponies or supper, except for Bowerman who had vanished back into the darkness beneath his little hill. Findhorn dismissed Caradoc's final question about Wolfsbane's remarkable powers of speech with the warning that he had better not seek to observe these powers at close quarters, as the badger was ill-tempered, unpredictable and not at all fond of Moorlanders. He then disappeared into the darkness to find Bowerman.

Several hours later, supper and its attendant chores complete, the entire complement of the Rings gathered before Bowerman's house. Wolfsbane had been persuaded to attend and, true to form, kept the whole group waiting some while before he and his four henchmen deigned to show up. Before the entrance to the mound lay a long, low granite table upon which Fortinbras spread his map. He explained for the benefit of Bowerman and the badgers the events leading to the moot at Buzzard Woods, the discussions taken there and the plan to meet again at Drizzlecombe.

Fortinbras then stepped forward and introduced Rufus, a tall, slightly round-shouldered figure and one of the Grimspounders freed by Wolfsbane. Thrust into the limelight by the elder, Rufus peered about him nervously and seemed lost for words.

"Well, get on with it," blustered Fortinbras unsympathetically.

"It was about a week ago," Rufus stammered reluctantly. "Two days after the solstice, I think. Our outriders reported that a large company of Simians was advancing down the river towards our mark.

"Our elder, and many of our warriors, were at Buzzard Woods," he went on with growing confidence, "and there was no time to get a message to them. Rather than allow them to attack our village we sent half of our available soldiers to meet them, the other half remaining to protect the village. I went with the forward party and Lemuella was our leader. You must have heard of her, she is our archery champion."

"I know her well," said Hyperica. "She was my pupil."

"We met them where the rivers meet," Rufus indicated the spot on the map, "and when we saw the size of their troupe we knew we had no chance. They were hundreds. Many rode on horseback wielding hogweed whips. Behind them advanced rank upon rank of foot soldiers armed with great pikes and sabres. And they were led by a creature, the mere sight of which spread terror in our hearts – a Simian like them, but of immeasurably greater size. Greater in size even than Bowerman he seemed, although we did not come to close quarters with him, as he drove his troops on from behind. Lemuella filled him full of arrows like a ten-foot hedgehog but still he came on and perhaps it was just our fear of him…"

Rufus again became distracted and he fell silent. Caradoc could see that he was shaking slightly. He saw signs of emotion also in the other Grimspounders. Fortinbras was plainly irritated by this lack of fortitude on the part of his fellow Moorlanders. He would not expect such weakness from Drizzlecombers, he announced, and urged the speaker either to continue or get out of his sight.

Findhorn had other ideas, and had already resolved to interrupt and complete the story himself from the account already given to him. Rufus' terror could become contagious. He told of the valiant Moorlander defence, the piles of Simian dead and the eventual collapse in the face of superior forces. Many Moorlanders had met their deaths but many more had been taken prisoner or had escaped back into the woodland, no doubt to regroup and continue their defence should the Simian patrol march on to the village.

The invaders had imprisoned their captives in wicker cages and then split into groups to mop up those who had escaped. Unfortunately for them, one group searching for fleeing Moorlanders had stumbled upon Wolfsbane and his friends instead. Findhorn bowed respectfully in the direction of Wolfsbane as if to invite him to continue the account. Wolfsbane grunted and stared pointedly in the opposite direction.

Instead, Fortinbras butted in again. "Well, that settles it, we must go to Grimspound. We leave now."

"I understand your concern," said Bowerman, speaking for the first time. "But there is no point. If the monkeys went on to the village, they will have reached it by now. I will send my buzzards for news."

"Monkeys did not go to village," contributed Wolfsbane unexpectedly. "Snivelling monkey tell me before he die. They go back way they came… or we kill them," he said as an afterthought.

"Well, that is good news at least," said Findhorn. "But I do not like the sound of their captain. I hope there are not more like him."

Bowerman could not hide the intensity of his interest in this new revelation but said nothing.

"In any event, I do not think this changes our plans significantly," went on Findhorn. "We must still meet at Drizzlecombe to decide whether to rescue our friends and if so, how? Only now, there will be more to rescue but if we do not act, then we may all need rescue. But, some of us should go via Grimspound and Fortinbras, if I may be so bold as to ask him, may wish to lead a small patrol there. They will be reassured to know we are still with them."

Findhorn paused for a second to allow his audience to absorb his comments, then mindful of the great Moorlander passion for democracy he enquired, "Are we agreed?" Arken and Fortinbras nodded, to be followed by most of the others. No one expressed dissent.

"Finally," said Findhorn, "I have some good news. Our friend Bowerman has agreed to help us. He has vowed to stick with us until there is an end of this matter and to accompany us into the very heart of the Northmoor if necessary."

Much relief and good humour greeted this announcement. Whatever great warriors the Lord of the Northmoor had at his disposal, his Moorlander foes surely had the greatest of them all. Bluffinch, peering in upon the deliberations from the edge of the circle, resolved that as Caradoc was now the bosom companion of the old wizard he, the foremost young warrior of the Buzzard Woods Mark, would soon become Bowerman's firm friend. The fact that they had not yet exchanged a single word did not seem to deter him.

"And, I am hopeful," concluded Findhorn with uncharacteristic hesitation, "that the adherence of one great warrior to our cause may now attract another." Everyone in the circle seemed to know exactly to whom this invitation referred, except its intended object. Whether the badger's attentions lay elsewhere or whether he was simply not terribly bright was not immediately apparent. Certainly no one believed that he would fail to identify himself as the other great warrior. The glare of nearly fifty eyes upon him gradually brought forth the realisation that a response was expected of him. He grunted a grunt that by now was well known to all, stood up and walked away.

CHAPTER TEN

A Strange Sea Creature and Home

By the time Caradoc awoke the following day, Fortinbras and his party had already left for Grimspound. The badgers too were long gone. Caradoc certainly did not miss the feeling of uneasiness generated by their unpredictable presence, much like that instilled by a large bully into a group of children, but he was still reassured when Findhorn announced that they had sworn to return at Drizzlecombe.

An hour later the remainder of the company wound its way back down the same narrow path they had ascended the previous day into the same mist. Caradoc wondered whether that mist, beautiful though it seemed, might hide the giant Simian or the bear or even both. The descent into the river valley took but a fraction of the time of the previous day's climb and before long the company was picking its way at leisurely pace through the water meadows. By mid-morning the mist had dispersed and the fresh, clear air promised a fine afternoon. Even old Neb had a spring in his gait, and so real was the universal optimism and good humour, that Bluffinch and Caradoc rode together chatting happily for some way. Caradoc began to think that perhaps Bluffinch was not such a bad fellow after all. He would rather have walked with Findhorn, of course, and as always had a hundred questions to ask him – Why could Wolfsbane talk? Where had he gone? And why was Bowerman not coming with them? would do for starters. But Findhorn was deep in conversation with his father so he would have to make do with Bluffinch.

After a while, their conversation exhausted, Caradoc begame distracted by the dragonflies. He had never seen so many – flashes of green and purple darting from tree to tree or hanging motionless over the water. He guided Neb gently off the path through the undergrowth and onto the rock-strewn bank, where he dismounted. Across the water in the shade of the weeping willows lining the eastern bank, an emerald monster attended by a host of courtier gnats, smaller dragonflies and blue damselflies loitered lazily a foot or so above the surface. This was truly a king amongst insects, thought Caradoc, a Bowerman amongst flies. If the Goddess had wished to create a perfect insect, this would be it.

A double thud to his left failed to break the spell but the heavy, uneven breathing that followed drew his gaze to a high, rounded boulder on the water's edge some ten feet away. His eyes fell upon two brown hairless feet and above them a form now becoming horribly familiar. The heavy breastplate and macabre face mask were those of his pursuers on Saddlemoor Down. Through the mask peered the intent Simian eyes, mean and small. As the creature realised what he had come across, his jaws fell open in an idiotic grin and he cackled a harsh, screeching laugh.

Caradoc did not immediately panic. His companions could not be far away and a loud holler would surely summon them. He threw back his head to yell but the sound seemed insignificant against the background noise of the fast-flowing river. The monkey grinned again as the full horror of the fact that he was alone dawned on his intended victim. Caradoc's first thought was flight but he had heard from Hama how fast these creatures moved and he feared he would be run down in seconds. The only thing for it was to stand and fight. He fingered the blade at his side, reluctant to draw it for fear of provoking an attack. But no provocation was needed. The laughter became a snarl and the Simian sabre flourished about the head of the beast.

What happened next stayed long in Caradoc's mind. The monkey bounded forward off the rock and appeared for a second to hang unsupported in the air. As Caradoc stared transfixed, the expression of devilish anticipation on its face changed to uncertainty and then to terror.

Two pairs of green spiderish arms enveloped the attacker from behind, held it rigidly for a moment and then, with frightening force, hauled the flailing body back across the boulder and plunged it below the waters. Caradoc caught a fleeting glimpse of a dull greenish grey mass hiding below the surface of the river. Afterwards he recalled the very stillness which followed. Despite its apparent size and obvious strength the creature in the river caused no disturbance of the water to speak of. There was no sign of a struggle. Only a few gentle ripples caressed the surface as it receded. And above the ripples the flight of the emerald monster with its myriad of tiny consorts marked the course of the creature as it retreated downstream towards the sea.

Caradoc had retained sufficient of his wits about him to withdraw for some minutes into the nearest undergrowth in case the Simian had not travelled alone. As soon as he was sure the coast was clear he re-emerged and slipped furtively back to the bank. He gazed downstream. There was nothing. Both the creature and the dragonflies had vanished. The gnats alone remained. Could they have come together? he wondered. He recalled tales he had heard around the village feasting table of the great leviathans of the southern seas whose submarine passage was tracked by hosts of voracious seabirds. Could this have been a leviathan of the river? For one ludicrous moment he almost felt sorry for the monkey. How impotent its malice had proved in the clutches of the creature.

He began to pick his way back to the path. To his relief Neb was awaiting him patiently, blissfully unaware of the drama that had unfolded only a few yards away. Bluffinch was nowhere to be seen. Caradoc remounted and set off down the path at a steady canter, drawn on by the eagerness to tell his tale while it was fresh in his mind. He had not gone far when he met his father and Narwhal coming back down the path to find him.

Arken's evident relief at the meeting suggested to his son that he might already know something of his story. But neither wished to waste time relating matters twice and Findhorn would have to know, so they quickly overhauled the rest of the party. Findhorn greeted his young friend warmly, to Caradoc's considerable pleasure. Obviously, his merciless interrogation of the old mage concerning all things new or strange had not entirely exhausted his patience. Caradoc knew it was inevitable that there was more of the same to come. His curiosity about the creature that had saved him was irrepressible.

As he had read in his father's face, the party had already encountered Simians. A small group of three or four had passed quite openly along a ridge above the opposite bank of the river. Their distance and numbers posed no threat but Arken had been alarmed at Caradoc's absence and set off back down the trail in search of him.

Findhorn then took up the story. "Fortunately," he explained, "it does not appear that the Simians sent out any outriders and so we have not come across any at close hand."

"Oh, but they did," exclaimed Caradoc triumphantly. "One attacked me."

Narwhal, riding alongside him, nearly fell off his pony in amazement. "What on earth happened?" he spluttered.

"Are you hurt?" chorused Arken and Findhorn together.

"Perhaps he fought it off," chimed in Bluffinch.

Bluffinch's presence and the rapt attention of every rider in earshot constituted a sore temptation to call Bluffinch's bluff and depict a titanic dual between Moorlander and Simian. But he glanced around at the honest, open faces of his companions and knew that their concern deserved better of him.

"Well, no, I'm not hurt and I didn't exactly fight it off. Someone else did." Caradoc saw that his answer had only served to increase his friends' surprise. "Well, some*thing* really," he continued.

"Yes, well, when you're ready, perhaps you'll tell us what," Findhorn snapped. "We don't have all day."

"But, I don't know what it was," he replied, flustered. "I didn't even really see it. It came out of the river and grabbed the monkey from behind just as it was about to spring."

Caradoc glanced back at Findhorn and was startled by the change in his demeanour. The irritation of a few moments ago had given way to intense interest.

"You must have seen more than that. What colour was it? What did it do?"

"It was green, I think, and it pulled the monkey into the water." Caradoc hesitated lest in his eagerness to please he recalled more than he had actually seen. "Then it vanished."

Findhorn could not disguise his excitement.

"Ha! That taught it," he yelped with the unrestrained

glee of a ten-year-old. Then, evidently abashed by this loss of composure, he added, "But we had better not continue up the valley in case others lie in wait for us ahead. We'll turn westward around the bottom of the moor and return to Buzzard Woods up the valley of the third river."

Although Caradoc could see the sense in this, he could also see that this new course would bring the company closer to Findhorn's cave in the limestone cliffs above the estuary of the third river. He therefore suspected that Findhorn had an ulterior motive.

Findhorn had forged ahead at the fore of the column away from the river and Caradoc took some time to catch up with him. As always, Findhorn seemed lost in thought and Caradoc resolved to plunge straight ahead with his questioning. The present was as good a time as any and he could cope with rejection.

"Isn't your home on the third river?" he enquired tentatively.

"Uh, what? Oh yes, but we aren't going anywhere near there."

"I just thought – well, I heard in the past – that you hadn't left your home for years before you came to the moot, and I thought you might be missing it."

Findhorn glanced at Caradoc with a look of some amusement. "Well, you heard that, did you? Who did you hear that from?"

"Oh, I can't remember," replied Caradoc, looking every bit as if he could remember despite the fact that he genuinely could not.

"Well, the thought is a most considerate one at any

rate," responded the Mage. "But your interpretation of my motives is a little off course. We will travel slightly northwest and cross the fourth river at Sequers Bridge. We will then skirt the Western Beacon and meet the third river as it begins to rise onto the moor. That will be some miles north of my little cave. But don't be too disappointed for me. It's true I don't leave my home often. I'm an old man and old men are best left at home. Anyway, I don't really have anywhere to go. All my friends and relations are either dead or went west years ago. At least by going this way, I won't have to protect you and all the other little Moorlanders from the bear."

Caradoc was not certain whether this remark was Findhorn's idea of humour at the expense of the Moorlander company. He resisted the temptation to point out that Findhorn had not done much to protect poor Romulus when last they encountered the bear. Having found the Mage so talkative he decided he was more interested in acquiring knowledge than scoring points and pressed on with his next question.

"You know what creature it was that saved me, don't you?"

"Am I so transparent?"

Caradoc had never met anyone less transparent. "Not usually," he said. "Usually I have no idea what you are thinking but you were excited by my tale."

"You will make a mage one day with such intuition," exclaimed Findhorn, oozing satisfaction. "Yes, I do think I know what manner of creature it was."

Caradoc felt a shiver of excitement run down his spine.

Was he to be taught the knowledge of the Mage? Would he learn the common tongue? Would he one day share with Findhorn his knowledge of the earth, its creatures and the spirit that ruled it? So certain was he of Findhorn's intentions that his thoughts moved to the practical. Would he spend months or even years with Findhorn at his cave to learn these things? That might be a little dull.

But nothing was further from Findhorn's thoughts, which remained with the sea creature. "You have caught a glimpse of indescribable antiquity," he said. "You may well be the only Moorlander now living to see what you have seen."

He listened enraptured as Findhorn recounted the history of the marine dwellers of the Western Isles, their civilisation and their ultimate demise. Never before had he heard the old man speak with such passion and with such apparent disregard for the passing of time. For the whole of that day's journey the tale continued and throughout the evening as they sat around the campfire. And even the crossing of the fourth river at mid-morning the following day and the approaching assent onto the moor did not diminish the enthusiasm of the teller. The rest of the company looked on and wondered what new wisdom the Mage had to impart and why he had chosen Caradoc as its recipient.

He told of a time when the Western Isles were much greater in number and stretched all along the southern coast and far out into the great ocean. With the passing of millennia and the rising of the oceans, few now remained. The ancestors of men and Moorlanders had dwelt upon these islands as had the ancestors of Bowerman – never great in numbers but far more plentiful than recently. And in the seas around these islands – warmer in those days – had dwelt the Armorici. The islands had been theirs alone before the coming of Moorlanders and men but, benign and wise, they had shared their lands with the newcomers – only withdrawing somewhat from the land and living more of their lives in the shallow seas, where they had always been happier. And as well as sharing their lands, they also shared their knowledge, for they were the oldest race on earth and therefore closest to the Goddess and their knowledge was great. Many of their skills had survived through the ages and they might properly have been called the first mages.

But much like the tragedy of a later age, not all men could be trusted to use their knowledge for the benefit of earth's creatures. Inevitably groups emerged, keen to impose their will on others. As with most creatures wholly good, the Armorici, who alone possessed the power to stop them, could not see ill in others and did nothing. They then began to war amongst themselves and used the skills of the Armorici to destroy one another. They poisoned their enemies and the land and last of all they poisoned the sea. The creatures of the sea died off and with them died the Armorici.

As the company passed from the plain of the river to the foothills of the moor on the afternoon of the second day after the departure from the Rings, Findhorn described the last death throes of the noble sea creatures.

"It is said," he told Caradoc, "that some went south

to the land that now bears their name. Others survived on the islands along the southern coast. And as a boy, my father told me of an island at the mouth of the fifth river where there lived an Armoricus centuries old."

"What did they look like?"

"I have never seen one," replied Findhorn, "but my father believed them to be large and powerful with many limbs. And what is more wonderful, they were of many colours – constantly changing, blue, green and silver like the sea itself. Or should I say they *are*, for I firmly believe that the creature that took the Simian was one of them."

"From the island at the mouth of the fifth river?"

"It must have been, for I have never heard of any other around these parts."

"Will I be able to thank it for saving me – and will it help us against the Simians?"

"I cannot say," answered Findhorn. "An Armoricus has power within his own domain, his own island, the rivers and the sea. I do not know what powers they have elsewhere. I do not believe he could help us and I think that if you want to thank him you must go to him."

Caradoc mused deeply about the Armorici and their fate as the company re-entered the great wood of the Southmoor. He wondered why creatures as great and good as the Gigantici and the Armorici had to fail. It seemed that all creatures who had close contact with man were destined to decline. And yet many men were good and kind. It was only when they congregated together in huge numbers that they seemed to forget the consequences of their actions.

Had it not been that every step brought him closer to home he could have felt extremely depressed. The scented smells of the lowland summer woods were intoxicating but for Moorlanders they did not compare with the fresh, clean air of the moorland valleys. By early evening the company had reached the rim of the valley within a valley which cradled their village. The babbling of the Badgerbrook welcomed the travellers home.

CHAPTER ELEVEN

DRIZZLECOMBE

Polycanthus, posted lookout at the southern end of the village, was first to hail them as they dragged their tired legs back into the valley. The sentry also seemed to be fulfilling the role of a goatherd. The mere presence of the goats in the village suggested that those who had stayed at home also had a tale to tell, as in safer times the herd would only be brought down off the moor in winter.

Whooping with pleasure at their return, Polycanthus skipped on ahead of them to call out a welcoming party, and by the time they reached the first dome, Ebenezer and the village elders had assembled to greet them and Gorbaduc was already hard at work in the preparation of an appropriate culinary masterpiece.

Findhorn and his father were soon closeted away with

Ebenezer in deep deliberation and Caradoc wasted no time in acquainting Rollo and Michaelmas with every intimate detail of the journey. He was disappointed to hear from Michaelmas that his mother was not there, but immensely relieved that she had left for Drizzlecombe in anticipation of the council rather than returning home to Grimspound. He had been looking forward to telling her of the heroics of her friend but this would have to wait.

The memory of that evening remained long in Caradoc's mind – the last he would spend in his own dear valley before the advent of great peril, although he did not know it at the time: the taste of Gorbaduc's delights, the smell of the evening flowers, the sound of the pipe, harp and timbrels of the village band, the touch of the hands of his friends as he reeled with them to the music, and the sight of their relaxed and happy faces. Perhaps it was the sense of danger shared that enhanced the evening. More likely it was the liberal helpings of Godolphin's Corma beer enjoyed by all who were permitted to drink it that did the trick; the old Moorlander's ability to create wonderful beer, wheaten and honeyed, was exceeded only by his capacity to drink it. Whatever the reason, Caradoc could not remember a jollier time and the short night was threatening to dissolve into dawn before the revelries ended.

Caradoc rose early on the morrow, although not before a number of his contemporaries who, from the din they were making, seemed intent on renewing the celebrations of the night before. Inexplicably there was not an adult to be seen, except Granny Grizabel who was busy cleaning away the debris. Caradoc recalled that she had been whooping it up with the best of them only a few hours previously.

"Where is everyone, Granny?" he enquired of the wrinkled reveller.

"Ah," she cackled with malicious pleasure, "some might say they be cormatose." With this, she fell about with such mirth that she appeared in severe danger of becoming cormatose herself. The pun unfortunately was lost on Caradoc who turned away in the certain belief that he would get no sense from this particular source. Her next comment regained his interest.

"But them had better be up d'rectly… them's leavin' today."

"Leaving? For where?"

"Why, for Drizzlecombe, course. The council meeting's there tomorrow."

"But why? The council wasn't to meet there until next month. Why have they brought it forward?"

"P'raps them all wants to get cormatose together." With this, the delight in her own wit became uncontrollable and other than enquiring whether she had taught a certain badger how to talk, Caradoc could see that this conversation had outlived its usefulness.

As he wandered back to their dome, he wondered whether he would be popular with his father if he woke him. Fortunately, he did not need to take the risk, as his father emerged blinking into the sunlight just as he reached the door.

"Am I coming to Drizzlecombe?" he asked. "It isn't far

and there can't be much danger." Caradoc was convinced that Arken would say no and had prepared himself for a big argument. He was pleasantly surprised by the response.

"Yes, yes, we've decided to take the same party who went south together with Ebenezer, and Polycanthus. I wasn't keen on the idea but for some reason Findhorn thinks you might come in useful."

"Why, what did he say?" stammered Caradoc excitedly, his mind full of thoughts of a mystical apprenticeship.

"Nothing, only that he'd like you to come. We're leaving in an hour. Oh, and Berengaria is back. She will come too." Berengaria was a year or so older than Caradoc. He liked her but had an uncomfortable impression that she was much cleverer than him. She had been away at the Grimspound Mark undergoing archery training. All Moorlander girls seemed to want to be archers. Caradoc didn't know why but they did seem better at it than the boys.

Arken said this whilst on the move and almost before he had finished he had disappeared in the direction of Ebenezer's dome.

Caradoc skipped off in the direction of the pony compound to prepare Neb for the journey. Narwhal and Berengaria were there before him, tending to their own mounts. Narwhal was also tending to Findhorn's, to whose service he had been seconded whilst Fortinbras was away. He would meet his master again at Drizzlecombe.

"Do you know why we are going so soon?" he enquired of his new friend. "I asked Granny Grizabel but I had no sense from her."

"Granny who?" beamed Narwhal with good-natured amusement. "Is she your granny?"

"Not likely," retorted Caradoc.

"She's everyone's granny really, so that must include you," remarked Berengaria.

"But whether she is or not, she couldn't tell me what all the hurry is about," Caradoc concluded, keen to get back to the subject.

"That's because she knows you wouldn't want her for your granny," said Berengaria. "I'd love to have her as mine, she's wild."

"Ah, well, it seems that the Simians and their master are moving more quickly than our elders thought. The raiding party which attacked Grimspound swept onwards south and west. I do not think they actually entered the valley. Perhaps they were too few after their losses at Grimspound but they devastated your herds on the open moor and laid waste the crops. Ebenezer led a patrol against them but they have done their work and made off across the moor. Messengers were sent on to Drizzlecombe to warn them the marauders were heading their way but they arrived too late and the damage was already done. The animal pounds were razed to the ground and the poor occupants driven headlong down into the valley, some falling to their deaths over the escarpment of the Dewerstone. But despite the open and unprotected situation of the village, the raiders did not proceed to attack it and swept on northwards over the moor."

"Why not, do you think?" enquired Caradoc.

"Perhaps they did not trust their strength but Findhorn

believes they had received a call northwards and that their master is now mobilising his forces."

"And that is why we are hastening to Drizzlecombe so soon?"

"That is why."

The departure of the company from the valley an hour or so later recalled to Caradoc's mind that similar recent exodus and the apprehension with which he had faced the forthcoming challenge. And yet compared with the perils which might lie ahead, the search for Bowerman had been child's play. The road to the Rings had led the party directly away from the source of the greatest danger and into the hands of friends. But even this had been fraught with peril and one of their number had not returned. Caradoc did not know where their course would now lead them but he knew they were heading northward – to Drizzlecombe and perhaps beyond. And northward lay the realm of Wistman and his Simian hordes. Thus mused Caradoc as the ponies picked their way out of the dwindling woodland and on to the open slopes of Penn Beacon. A glance around at his companions betrayed their shared fears as rider after rider steadied his mount and turned to take a last lingering look at the secure and friendly woodland stretching away into the distance behind them. A few hundred yards further and the vista opened out beyond the rolling green treetops onto the water meadows of the lowlands beyond. Despite the scattered pale grey cloud, the air was bright and clear and Caradoc could clearly espy the distant shimmering silver of the sea. To the west, the great bay in whose depths merged the waters of six rivers loomed large against the horizon. Many of the company who gazed down that day looked upon the sea for the first time. A few wondered whether they would do so again.

Eventually and reluctantly the company turned its back on the friendly south and forged ahead over the high moor. The course to Drizzlecombe lay north-northwest over some of the highest and most open ground of the Southmoor. Findhorn's plan was to negotiate the lofty pile of Shell Top and then to detour somewhat to the west to avoid the even more substantial dome of Shavercombe. Thus it was hoped to reach the valley of the second river by dusk. Caradoc shared the Mage's reluctance to pass the night on the open moor, particularly as he had recognised the slopes of Penn Beacon as the site of his confrontation with the marauding band of Simians. It seemed an age ago, yet only a few weeks had passed.

A red and liquid sunset was dissolving over the hills beyond the great river before the company began the descent into the river valley. Camp was struck and tired legs were dangled in the cool water of the river whilst supper was prepared. Caradoc sat on the bank with Narwhal, Berengaria and Bluffinch, relating again the tale of the chase on Saddlemoor Down. Caradoc noticed that Bluffinch seemed reluctant to exercise his powers of sarcasm in the presence of Berengaria whose own powers of sarcasm were legendary. Bluffinch seemed a little in awe of her. He seemed less inclined to ridicule the incident now that danger was really at hand. Narwhal explained that the waters of the second river flowed straight to the great South Western Bay. He wondered whether the sword-nosed fish swam in that bay. Caradoc wondered if Armorici dwelt there.

To both at that instant it seemed a far more desirable destination than any which might lie on the northern banks of the river. And yet, that night Caradoc could not sleep for excitement about Drizzlecombe. Moorlander civilisation had never spawned a larger community, and tomorrow it would be swollen to even greater size with visitors from every mark and others come to aid the common cause. Caradoc's mental image of the Moorlanders' capital grew vaster, yet vaguer, as drowsiness became sleep. When he awoke the following morning, the image still lingered with him.

The company made no excessive haste to break camp on the morrow as the distance was not great and the Drizzlecombe Council would not meet until late afternoon. Their route took them away from the river, along the edge of the same Shavercombe ridge from which they had descended the previous day. Caradoc could not detect the reason as the way seemed more difficult.

"Why are we going this way?" he enquired of his father. "I prefer the river to the moor. Are there fish in it?"

"That's two questions," smiled his father, "but both are easy to answer. There are many fish in the river – salmon, trout, perch and even the odd pike."

Caradoc shuddered, despite the fact that his childhood fear of pike seemed rather foolish in the light of the current peril. The ludicrous thought crossed his mind that the company had been driven away from the river by pike.

"And, we have come this way to avoid the bog," continued his father. "All the riverbank on both sides between Hen Tor and Ringmoor Down is bog. There are few of us enough as it is and we don't want to lose anyone in the mire."

Caradoc gazed riverwards across the sleek green bed of moss – beautiful and treacherous – through which they could not pass. Scattered tufts of sedge grass waved hesitantly on the faltering breeze and a marsh pippet piped thinly from the opposite bank; delicate asphodel peeped demurely out from between the grasses. Caradoc did not think the bog looked at all dangerous and said so. Findhorn, who had drawn up alongside on his old nag as they spoke, overheard them. "You would be most unwise to put that view to the test," he advised. "My father once told me a grim tale of the great mires at the river's head. My father's brother and his friend were crossing the moor from the Moorland Way to your mark at Buzzard Woods. The friend was an ancient moorman who knew every inch of the Southmoor and the two picked their way, leading their ponies behind them from turf to turf through the bog. They had passed the centre and were in sight of the far side when my uncle pointed out to his friend a small dark object lying on the moss some twenty-five yards ahead. From a distance it resembled on upturned pail but as they drew nearer it revealed itself as a hat. My uncle stooped and raised it. To his eternal amazement a head was revealed stuck fast in the mire which turned indignantly towards him.

"''Ere, that's my hat,' protested the captive.

"'Well, I'm very sorry to disturb you, I'm sure,' replied my uncle. 'I hadn't realised you were underneath it.'

"'For certain I be,' retorted the head, apparently without any great desire to be anywhere else, 'and so's my hoss.'

"The two travellers looked around them for the unfortunate beast but seeing nothing, and believing the man to have been driven mad by his ordeal, my uncle's friend humoured him by saying, 'Oh yes, I see.'

"''Ow can you possibly see him, when I be sittin' on 'im?' fairly bawled the fellow.

"'Sitting on him?' spluttered my uncle.

"'Well of course I'm sittin' on 'im, what else would I be doin' with me hoss when I'm ridin' 'im?'

"It seemed that he had been foolish enough to attempt to cross the area on horseback – an impossible task even with much friendlier mires – and horse and rider had sunk up to the man's neck."

During the latter stages of his tale, Caradoc had examined Findhorn's countenance closely for any hint of humour but had detected none. Both Arken and Findhorn appeared deadly serious and yet neither displayed the look of horror which Caradoc would have expected on the face of one exposed to this dreadful history for the first time.

"Nonsense," he exclaimed, "I don't believe a word of it."

Both adults turned their heads simultaneously and looked balefully towards him. As they did so, the realisation struck him that he had slowly drifted up hill away from the river and there was now some twenty or so yards between himself and his fellow riders.

Caradoc was still lost in profound contemplation of the horror of the moorland mire when an hour or so later, the company rounded a granite outcrop below Hen Tor. A breathtaking panorama opened out before them to the north; the valley of the second river wound its sinuous way into the heart of the Southmoor. On the near side of the river, the still-boggy bank formed a narrow border some twenty or so feet wide between the river and the western escarpment of the moor. On the wide expanse of riverbank opposite sprawled the largest collection of dwellings Caradoc had ever seen. The immediate banks of the river were empty save for two great rows of menhirs running roughly parallel to the water. Between these silent stone giants and the village itself, the gently rising bank was fairly pickled with makeshift dwellings rapidly assembled to house the busy hordes flooding in from the other marks. Above and beyond this ramshackle shanty town, a wide-bottomed coombe receded into the distance at right angles to the valley of the river. All along the lower slopes of the coombe side lay the permanent domes of the Moorlander capital. Caradoc had never previously looked upon the dwellings of his people from a distance, the domes of the other villages being camouflaged by their leafy settings, and he was quite startled by their appearance. To fend off harsh moorland winds, the Drizzlecombe builders were wont to envelope the granite walls and thatched roofs of their domes with turfs of greater thickness than those employed by their Buzzard Woods counterparts. The dense grassy covering leant them the appearance of

112

huge green molehills, strangely distorted by the contours of the granite boulders beneath the surface.

The entire valley was alive, bustling with innumerable tiny figures scurrying to and fro. The animal pounds on the upper slopes of the coombe bulged with horses and ponies of every size and shape, and fluttering over the whole scene a myriad of flags and pennants flourished in a blaze of colour.

Caradoc's total absorption in the spectacle across the river was disturbed by Bluffinch. "There must be thousands of them. We'll teach those ugly apes a lesson they won't forget."

Caradoc did not immediately reply. Increasingly as the journey had progressed he had begun to think that perhaps Bluffinch was not so bad after all and the sentiments he had expressed had been going through his own mind at that moment. But the complete certainty of Bluffinch's opinion brought home to Caradoc the folly of overconfidence. He strained his eyes in the hope of picking out some larger figures amongst the thousands.

"Are they all Moorlanders?" he asked Bluffinch. "I wonder if Bowerman or the badgers are there."

"We don't need their help," was the predictable reply.

"I wouldn't tell them that," said Berengaria. Caradoc glanced at her approvingly and then as if to reinforce his own uncertainties and anxieties his gaze drifted beyond Drizzlecombe northwards. To the west of the coombe, a mile or two distant, rose the rounded rocky brow of Sheepstor now bathed in reassuring sunshine. Caradoc knew that behind the tor on the shores of the moor's greatest lake lay the village of the fourth mark, now no doubt yielding many of its inhabitants to the multitude thronging the opposite bank.

Immediately to the north of the coombe beyond the patchwork of little fields, a range of low, round, green tors lay similarly bathed in sunshine. His eyes scanned beyond them and their course northward was blocked by a long, dark bank of the deepest blue which Caradoc first mistook for cloud. But the jagged points rising skyward above the lowering mass betrayed its density. This was no cloudbank but the tors of the Northmoor glaring down upon the softer contours of the South from a great height.

Caradoc shuddered. He wondered what eyes might scrutinise the tiny scurrying figures far below at that very moment – and with what intent. Perhaps Simian scouts spied upon their preparations, laying bare all their futile schemes and reporting back to their masters. Perhaps even their masters looked on – the giant Simian of the Grimspound raid, if he had survived Lemuella's arrows, or the Lord of the Northmoor himself.

The northern sky besported a deeper, darker blue even than the tors themselves as if the very sunlight itself declined to rest upon their rugged heights. But even as he gazed, the clear border between dark and light ran rapidly up the southern escarpment of the Northmoor, plunging the tor summits into brilliant sunshine. Perhaps even now the watchers were scattering headlong in panic and burying themselves in deep, dark caves far from the light.

The realisation dawned that Bluffinch was still talking. It said much about his companion, he thought, that his conversation forged onwards regardless of the absence of any interested audience. The rest of the company, similarly unenthralled by Bluffinch's conversation, had moved downhill towards a ford roughly opposite the most southerly menhir. A few had already crossed to the other side. Caradoc set off after them.

CHAPTER TWELVE

NEW FRIENDS

There was nothing else in the world quite like Drizzlecombe – well, nothing in the world known to the Moorlanders at any rate. Caradoc quickly slipped away from Bluffinch and disappeared into the throng to explore. He would locate his friends later. All about him was bustle and activity. On the flat ground along the river, gangs of dexterous builders rapidly erected temporary huts to house the hordes of visitors. Caradoc looked on transfixed as in less than ten minutes a gang of seven artisans compiled an entire hut. Two constructed the circular lower walls of smooth granite boulders. Two more piled on the upper walls of densely packed earth. A fifth arranged the oak poles, sunk in the earth at the outer edge and meeting in a pinnacle at the centre, while the sixth and seventh bound them fast together with a twine of rushes and bindweed. The huts lacked the earth-packed double-leaved walls and the reed-thatched roofs of the permanent domes or the shelter walls to protect the doorway from the sharp moorland winds but they were undoubtedly preferable to a night on the open moor.

Between the cluster of temporary dwellings and the village itself lay a veritable manufactory of artisans conceiving, designing and crafting a multitude of wares, from swords and shields of the toughest bronze to delicate bejewelled headbands in exquisite wood. One gaunt and grizzled potter sat on a grassy hillock tending his wheel surrounded by piles of pots, some recently completed and others the work of earlier, less perilous, days, offered for sale. Caradoc peered from a respectful distance in the hope of picking out one adorned with a long-nosed fish. Alongside him a burly, bearded weaponsmith tested a great longbow, its string drawn for the first time, taut across his chest. And amongst them all a host of entertainers – dancers, jugglers, musicians and bards – soothed the artisans through their labours.

Caradoc's attention was drawn to a cross-legged harpist at the centre of a circle of eager listeners, her long black tresses almost entirely enveloping her harp strings. Her song told the story of the founding of the Drizzlecombe Mark – the oldest of the four and the proudest. The tale, more a legend than a history, spoke of the coming of the ancestors of the Drizzlecombers in round, skin-clad coracles up the moorland rivers. Caradoc was about to join the bard's seated audience when a shrill voice stopped him in his tracks.

"Oi… hog face… Wanna be an oldun?"

Caradoc turned quickly. Beneath a pile of granite boulders sat three young Moorlanders – older than himself but not by much. The dispenser of the insult was a scuffy bristle-headed fellow – an urchin, Grandma Grizabell would have called him.

"Eh, what do you mean?" Caradoc asked and then, remembering the insult, he said pointedly, "And who are you calling hog face? There are uglier creatures in the world than hogs, you know."

"You were listening to those old songs she sings for the olduns," retorted the bristlehead. "We're going caving."

These words were uttered with an air of hostility but Caradoc suspected that their speaker was prompted more by boredom with his present company than by malice and resolved to take up the challenge.

"Caving… where and for what?" There was a brief silence. The bristlehead looked distinctly uncomfortable.

"Ha ha! He can't say it," spluttered a gaunt, round-shouldered companion with undisguised glee.

"Course I can, I've just forgot it, that's all."

"Ha ha," continued the gaunt companion, whose mirth was now becoming uncontrollable. The object of his humour looked on aggressively.

"Well, what is it then?" Caradoc pressed impatiently.

The third of the group, who he now noticed that, despite sporting hair shaved almost as close as the bristlebonse – it must be the fashion round these parts, he thought – was a girl, came to his assistance.

"You won't get any sense from old Lungwort," she

exclaimed, gesturing towards the tongue-tied bristlehead. "We're hunting for osmundacea. Do you know what that is?"

Caradoc wanted to say yes but feared they might invite him to explain.

"No – but I think I have heard of it before."

"It's a magical moss that creates its own light and cures all manner of ailments. It grows in caves. The Sheepstor herbalists buy it from us. Coming with us?" she asked.

Caradoc was doubtful. "How far is it?" he asked. "Mightn't we meet Simians?"

"About three miles. It isn't dangerous. We won't see any Simians. The whole area's crawling with our soldiers."

"When are you going?"

"Straight away, otherwise we won't be back before dark."

"Shouldn't we tell someone where we're going?" asked Caradoc.

"Don't be daft. They wouldn't let us."

Caradoc had no time to enquire why, if it wasn't dangerous, anyone would wish to stop them, as it was evident that the others were about to set off. Not wanting to appear timid in the eyes of this dictatorial girl, he resolved to come along.

"What about my pony?" he shouted after them.

"Don't worry, you can borrow Old Boney."

Caradoc scampered off in their wake and reached the pony pound just as Bluffinch was leaving with Polycanthus, having bedded their ponies down for the evening.

"Hello, Caradoc," beamed Bluffinch cheerily. "Where are you off to?"

Caradoc was having difficulty in coming to terms with this new bonhomie between himself and his old adversary, and was eager to quash any suggestion that he might accompany them.

Before he could devise an appropriately evasive reply, Lungwort butted in.

"Goin' cavin' to make some money. Comin'?"

The bossy girl to whom it had immediately occurred that the greater the numbers the lesser each share of the spoils, earned Caradoc's unending gratitude by interjecting.

"No, he ain't. Too many tramping feet will frighten off the moss. Come on, hurry up."

Caradoc was all confusion. Could this moss walk? There was no time to ask, as the others had already retrieved their ponies from the pound and were making their way between the domes to the northern edge of the village.

Caradoc shrugged his shoulders in Bluffinch's direction with a show of insincere disappointment. But the look of concern on Polycanthus' face was far from insincere. Caradoc had always liked Polycanthus despite the fact that he did not know him particularly well. The tall, rather gawky, young Moorlander was several years older than Caradoc and yet not quite an adult. At least he had that amiable and unassuming disposition that invited Caradoc and his contemporaries to treat him as an equal. It was reputed that he could run like the wind and never get tired but Caradoc had never seen anything more than a canter.

"It may be none of my business, old chap, but does Arken know where you're off to… and where are you off to?"

"Well, no, I haven't asked him, but he won't mind," said Caradoc.

"It isn't far… a few hundred yards that way." He pointed vaguely northwards. "And it won't be dangerous, the countryside's full of our soldiers."

"Well, take care anyway and I wouldn't go out of sight of the village."

Caradoc assured him he wouldn't and scampered off after his new friends. By the time he caught up with them they had already reached the edge of the village. He was pleased to see the talkative girl at the rear of the group. Bossy and balding she might be but she was pretty with it.

"What's your name?" he asked.

"Cloudberry. What's yours?" He told her.

She was leading two ponies, one of whom could be no other than Old Boney.

"You don't expect me to ride him, do you?" said Caradoc ungratefully. "He'll collapse."

"No he won't," replied Cloudberry. "He's stronger than he looks. He can carry Lungwort."

Caradoc glanced ahead at the burly bristlehead, who surely outweighed the scrawny beast, and hoped resolutely that this claim would not have to be put to the test.

As the group wound its way slowly northwards and westwards in the direction of three jagged peaks to the north of Sheepstor, Caradoc chatted away merrily with Cloudberry. He found her an absorbing companion. She and her little group were obviously a constant source of irritation to the more respectable members of Drizzlecombe society, and Caradoc was enthralled by the tales of ingenious mischiefs perpetrated upon the hapless adults of the village and sometimes often their own contemporaries. Tales abounded of dining table pony pats cunningly disguised as chocolate pudding and pot-bellied moorland porkers sporting monkey masks skilfully designed for them by her own hand. Even some of the grown-ups had seen the funny side of this jape at first. Later, as the danger became more real, the monkey-faced pigs had seemed less amusing.

By the time Caradoc's enthusiasm for Cloudberry's drolleries had begun to wane, the group had placed some one and a half miles between themselves and the village. Looking back, the southern reaches of the river valley could be seen winding away into the distance but both the nearer reaches and the village itself were obscured from view. Caradoc remembered the advice of Polycanthus but reassured himself that, despite the absence of the expected hordes of Moorlander soldiers, they must be about somewhere.

A few hundred yards further and the three jagged peaks Caradoc had espied as they had left the village loomed up on their left. They seemed less lofty and intimidating now, the path from Drizzlecombe having risen gently to a ridge which joined the three peaks to the higher land at the centre of the moor. The land to the northwest of the ridge fell way into a great basin bound on three sides by the moor itself. To the west, however, the land continued to fall away almost as far as the eye could see, which in the clear light of a late summer afternoon was a great distance. Caradoc fancied he could just pick out the peaks of other hills far into the west, but he could not be sure.

His gaze was drawn northwards by the words of Cloudberry.

"Look, a storm over the Northmoor."

The northern wall of the basin was the huge escarpment of the Northmoor itself. But the granite peaks which had constituted Caradoc's first view of the dark land from the distant banks of the second river were now wholly lost in a pall of cloud of the deepest purple – deeper by far than the purple hue of the heather-clad slopes in the still-sundrenched basin far below.

"How much further?" he enquired of Cloudberry. "We don't want to end up in that."

"Oh, don't worry about that. It won't come down here. There's always a storm on the Northmoor."

Cloudberry could see that Caradoc was unconvinced. "Anyway, it's not far. Look down there."

She pointed a little to the west of due north and Caradoc was just able to pick out the outline of a small weirdly shaped tor a mile or so downhill.

"The moss is in the caves underneath."

"It looks a bit like a head… a huge ugly head… just standing there on a slope," said Caradoc nervously.

"Yes," chuckled Cloudberry. "A bit like Lungwort's."

As the group moved downhill towards the head-shaped tor, Caradoc kept a cautious eye on the path of the storm. At times the cloudbank appeared to advance some distance down the side of the escarpment. At others, it appeared, if anything, to have receded. Despite the failing light, the others showed no concern whatsoever. As the sinister-looking tor loomed up before them, Caradoc reassured himself with the thought that they had been here before and must know what they were doing.

The terrain at the base of the tor became increasingly difficult and the foragers were obliged to skip from boulder to boulder in single file. The bright green rushes between the boulders spoke of bog and Caradoc wondered whether his resourceful new friends could find their way back through it without the light.

CHAPTER THIRTEEN

VIXANA

The base of the tor was riddled with caves. Indeed the whole edifice was eaten away by a network of tunnels, which accounted for its strange contours. Cloudberry led the group into several before she found one to her satisfaction – a dark dank grotto sloping gently downhill into the bowels of the tor.

"This is the one," exclaimed Cloudberry adamantly.

"How can you tell?"

"The smell."

Caradoc inhaled. The odour was unmistakable: sickly sweet with a hint of violet.

"I've never smelt moss like that before."

"That's not the moss," chimed in Lungwort, eager to appear as moorwise as his friend. "That's a toadstool that grows by the moss, but don't eat it, don't even touch it, it's deadly."

"Eat it… I couldn't even see it in this darkness."

"You will when we reach it."

The group stumbled on, slowly feeling their way along the slimy wet walls. As they descended deeper, the temperature dropped and the sweet smell became more intense. Caradoc began to wonder whether they could possibly find their way back but Cloudberry reassured him that this particular cave was one long tunnel with one other leading off it – and that went upwards – so even the most stupid Grimspounder could not get lost there.

A dim glow beckoned at the end of the tunnel.

"Is that the other side of the hill?" Caradoc enquired hopefully.

"No, it's the moss."

When it first appeared, the light had seemed a considerable distance away but it plainly was not, as within a few strides further they could discern a gently illuminated chamber at the tunnel's end. As Caradoc stepped inside it he was astounded by its size. He imagined that he stood in a lighted hall within a hollow mountain. He surveyed the walls for flaming torches but there were none.

"Look… over here," bellowed Lungwort excitedly. "Masses of it."

The others ran to join him. A rocky promontory protruded over the western edge of the chamber. Around it was entwined, like strings of pearls, an embroidery of delicate filaments from which emanated a pale but clear light. The spectacle reminded Caradoc of an immeasurably long glow worm and he half expected it to uncoil and slither away across the floor of the cave. In the pools of light cast by the moss grew the source of the sickly smell: clumps of the pure white fungus, looking so fragile and fine that the slightest movement would reduce it to powder. Caradoc was astounded that something so beautiful could be so deadly. He looked on in awe, mesmerised. Lungwort, on the other hand, was wholly unimpressed by the vision. He was busily tearing the filaments of moss from their rocky roots and bundling them into bags brought for this purpose.

"Come on, give us a hand," he growled at Caradoc. "We didn't just bring you for the ride."

Cloudberry and the third Drizzlecomber, Dogberry, were already busy at work. Caradoc was gripped by a great reluctance to assist. Immediately the moss was ripped from the rock its light went out. He felt that he did not want to be part of this vandalism, whatever benefit there might be to the Sheepstor herbalists. He thought of attempting to put a stop to the desecration and he had even begun to contemplate the best means of imposing his will on the three burly Drizzlecombers when another came to his aid.

"And who gave you permission to steal my jewels, my little ones?"

The soft, rich, sympathetic female voice echoed around the walls of the chamber. The three gatherers froze. Caradoc turned and looked towards the voice. At first, peering from light into darkness, he could make out nothing. As if to assist them, the voice spoke again.

"Here I am, my dappled darlings. Look for me where the icicle falls."

Along the eastern wall of the chamber, some fifty or so feet away, a huge stalactite plunged groundwards, looking every bit a giant icicle. Beneath, on a granite slab akin to that on which they stood, sat a tall female figure, so tall in fact that as the eyes of the gatherers adapted to the light, they were gripped with an inexplicable sense of fear.

"We're sorry, we did not know they were yours," spluttered Cloudberry.

"Oh but they are," oozed the voice, "and this is my cave."

"But how were we to know?" joined in Caradoc defensively. "And who are you anyway?" he added with more confidence.

The woman now rose and smiled. She was tall indeed, taller than any female of the race of men that Caradoc had ever seen, yet not wholly intimidating. She was not young but Caradoc would not have described her as middle-aged either and as she moved slowly towards them her body, concealed beneath long robes of the palest green, seemed to glide effortlessly over the cavern floor.

The group backed away as she approached.

"You need not fear me, my little ones. Your parents would tell you so, were they here. I am the provider of treats for all children."

None of the group considered themselves children but no one was inclined to take issue with her, especially as the idea of a treat had certain attractions.

"And treats I will provide for you, my little guests," she positively cooed.

"Within my caves there grow giant golden mosses which are to these as buzzards are to wrens – mosses whose glow would illuminate the Northmoor in the depth of winter. Would my little friends look upon them?"

"They would… we would," exclaimed Lungwort, his fear now overcome by excitement.

"Um, can you tell us who you are first?" prompted Caradoc.

The woman, who had until now addressed the group collectively, now turned her attention upon Caradoc.

"Why, don't you know me?" she flashed with a hint of irritation and then, composing herself, she continued.

"Have not we undertaken many adventures together, my fickle friend?"

Caradoc was speechless. What could she mean? And then to his astonishment the face before him transformed. The features were the same – those of the smiling and slightly sinister woman of the cave – but the expression was unmistakably that of his dear mother.

He mouthed the word "Mother" but no words came, and as he did so, the expression faded and was gone.

The woman turned away. "Come," she said and his three companions obeyed. Caradoc could do no other than follow.

The woman led them back into the tunnel and then via a number of smaller tunnels into the heart of the tor. She carried with her a small lump of the shining moss to illuminate the way. So enthralled with her presence were they that it did not appear strange that the moss shone in her hands but not in theirs. Caradoc knew only that they were rising slowly and wondered whether they would attain the summit. And then he sensed fresh air – the cool, clear breeze of a moorland evening. A minute or so later they emerged onto the upper slopes of the tor. How the weather had changed. They could see nothing. The great cloudbank hanging over the Northmoor had descended onto the lower tor in the form of an opaque moorland mist, and had it not been for the breeze and the cold drizzle upon his face Caradoc would not have known that they had left the cave.

Caradoc searched desperately for the light. He fancied he glimpsed it a little way off. He called for his friends: "Cloudberry, Lungwort, where are you?"

"We're over here, dear, come, follow us." The voice was his mother's.

"Mother, Mother, is that really you?"

"Yes, this way, my dear."

He stumbled in the direction of the voice. His eagerness to meet his mother overcame his anxiety and he staggered forward towards the sound. A few paces onwards and he saw again the pale glow of the moss flickering and dancing as the moorland breeze blew into a wind and threatened to become a storm. But as the drizzle intensified and the mist thickened, the light rapidly dissolved and, fearful of losing it altogether and plunging into darkness, Caradoc quickened his pace.

A minute or so later the light had vanished entirely and Caradoc could follow it no further. He stopped and stood in the pitched darkness, straining his ears for a familiar voice above the rising wind.

"Cloudberry, Lungwort," he called and then querulously, "Mother." He could barely hear his own voice above the storm; he could not expect anyone else to do so. He was about to forge onwards when his call was answered by a cry that froze his blood. It began like a howling of the wind – thin and desperate – rose to a terrified scream and ended in a sickening thud.

Caradoc's unease now rose to panic. The sound had appeared to come from the direction in which he was heading. Did it emanate from some bloodthirsty demon pouring forth its savagery into the moorland night or was it the anguished cry of his companions in peril? Should he run towards the sound or flee from it? He chose the former. If some fell creature were abroad it would not find him in this darkness – unless he ran into it – and if his companions were in danger he must help them. He moved on furtively, feeling his way forward and shielding his face as he went against the pounding rain. He had covered only a few yards when his progress was brought to an abrupt halt. A strong arm encircled his neck and held him fast.

Caradoc had no time for fear. He grabbed at the arm and struggled furiously to cast it off. Then to his amazement he heard a familiar voice.

"Hold on, old chap. We've come to bring you back." The voice was unmistakably that of Polycanthus. "Come… this way."

"No, not that way, we've got to help the others," Caradoc remonstrated. "I heard…"

"No, old chap," Polycanthus interrupted. "There's nothing that way. We must go back down."

"But I heard a cry."

"Show him, Ellie."

Polycanthus appeared to address this remark to pitched darkness. But as if summoned by his words, a second figure materialised from behind him – a slight, elfin figure whose outline was illuminated by the dull light of a marsh lamp. The figure skipped nimbly forward a few paces and held the lamp aloft.

"Follow her," said Polycanthus quietly, "but take care and go no further."

Caradoc stepped gingerly forward and peered outward beyond the light. At his feet was bare granite, extending for a few feet. Beyond was nothing. He moved one pace further toward the granite edge and peered downwards. Once again, there was nothing.

Caradoc felt sick to the stomach. He knew now the significance of the bloodcurdling cry. It was the cry of one of his poor companions – which one he did not know – as he or she staggered blindly off the granite cliff and hurtled toward the moorland floor far below. And he also knew that he had come within a few feet of joining them. He buried his face in his hands and wept. The good-natured Polycanthus approached and embraced him.

"Come on, old chap, it was a close call but you're safe now."

Quickly recalling that Polycanthus' companion was a girl, he composed himself.

"Who was it that fell?" he enquired after a brief pause.

"Well, it wasn't that idiot Lungwort. We found him wandering about, blubbering, further down the hill." The girl spoke for the first time. Her tone was lively but unsympathetic. Caradoc wondered whether she felt the same contempt for him as she obviously felt for Lungwort. At least his distress could be interpreted as sorrow for his companion rather than fear for himself. Lungwort had no such excuse.

"It must be Cloudberry or Dogberry," said Polycanthus. "Pray to the Goddess that it wasn't both of them."

"No... I'm sure it was only one cry," replied Caradoc.

"Come on, let's get going, we'll call out as we go."

The three linked hands to avoid the risk of separation. The girl led the way, holding the marsh lamp aloft before her, and every ten yards or so Polycanthus called the names of the missing Moorlanders. There was no response. Whether their calls were drowned by the din of the storm or whether the object of their search had wandered out of earshot they could not tell but slowly their hope began to fade.

About halfway down the hill, the light of the marsh lamp disclosed a large hollow edged on three sides by granite walls. A thin path formed the fourth side of the dell and before undertaking its perilous negotiation, the three halted.

"Come on, chaps, let's make one last effort. Let's give it all we've got," exhorted Polycanthus.

Together they threw back their heads and bellowed the names of their friends into the storm.

"Cloudberree... Dogberree."

As the last prolonged syllables died on the wind, Caradoc's senses were assailed by two new stimuli at once. A flash of sheet lightning illuminated the northern sky. The summit of the tor on which they had just stood loomed up vast and forbidding. And as if the lightning itself had scent, the hollow filled with the same sickly sweet smell that haunted the hollow heart of the hill.

"It's the smell of the white fungus," Caradoc whispered uneasily.

"No," said Ellie, "it's the smell of the witch."

And so it was. With the very next flash of lightning they espied her seated above them on the south wall of the dell. Ellie raised the lamp towards her. She did not remind Caradoc of his mother now. The figure turned to meet the light and although the expression on the face was a smile, it was a smile replete with menace. The witch, for such she was, her knees clasped to her chin, rocked backwards and forwards, looking very like some enormous oscillating crow. And as she rocked, she growled – a low, thin growl like that of a small cat.

The three Moorlanders stood in silence for seconds expecting some dreadful stroke. But the witch remained leaning maliciously towards them – and rocking.

"What shall we do?" whispered Caradoc. "Do you think she has Cloudberry or Dogberry?"

Mere seconds passed as his companions appeared to consider a reply, and still the witch did no more than growl and rock.

"What do you think, Ellie?" asked Polycanthus indecisively. "Has she a captive? Why does she do nothing?"

"No, I don't believe she has and even if she does, we can't help now. We couldn't find anyone inside the tor. We must go now. I think she is in some kind of trance, brought on by the fungus. It may not be so easy to escape once she comes round."

"But what about the others?" exclaimed Caradoc indignantly. "We can't just leave them here."

"Hush, you fool… if she wakes, none of us will be leaving. We can come back with help."

Caradoc was now convinced that she did indeed hold him in the same contempt as Lungwort. But he could see the sense in her words. He followed her as she picked her way carefully along the narrow path bordering the hollow and onto the broader slopes beyond. As he passed over the rim of the hollow, he glanced back. The tall, gaunt figure remained perched on the ledge in the same hunched position – but now it was motionless.

After ten minutes or so of slow progress over the rocks, the descent began to flatten and they walked again on boggy ground. Again they linked hands and picked their way carefully between the little hillocks of solid ground. The resourceful Ellie, who had plainly walked these paths many times before, led the way and Caradoc followed. He thought how surprisingly smooth were her hands when compared with her abrasive nature. But perhaps she was not really so bad, perhaps she was just nervous.

After a few minutes he realised that they were drifting back uphill.

"Where are we going? Back to the tor?"

"We've got to collect your stupid friends," snapped Ellie.

"They aren't my friends," retorted Caradoc, and then, feeling slightly guilty at disowning those with whom he had so recently shared great peril, he added, "Well, not old ones anyway."

"But old enough to want to save?"

"Oh yes, of course. We must help them," conceded Caradoc.

The girl smiled condescendingly. She was plainly accustomed to getting the better of the slower-witted young male Drizzlecombers.

Within a few moments, the anxious cries of the distraught Lungwort became clearly audible above the still-pounding wind. Ellie could not disguise her exasperation.

"The fool," she sneered, "he'll bring the witch down on us all."

"Have a heart, Ellie," said Polycanthus, "the poor fellow's probably frantic with worry in case we miss him."

The girl was plainly unimpressed. "Well, there's not much risk of that with him making that din." She was proved right, for a few yards further on a windswept and bedraggled Lungwort practically ran straight into her. Ellie was not his favourite Drizzlecomber but at least she was a familiar face, and Lungwort hugged her with uncontrollable relief and then Caradoc and Polycanthus in turn. And then with heavy hearts for their missing friends, the group turned for home.

CHAPTER FOURTEEN

THE OLD MAN IN
THE WOOD

When Caradoc awoke the next day it was already
mid-afternoon. He rose to much news, some
good and some bad. Amongst the good news
was that Cloudberry too had found her way back to the
village. She had staggered into the valley in a frightful state
an hour or so after the return of the others. By the time of
her return, Caradoc and Lungwort were already oblivious
to the world in the depths of blissful slumber but the rescue
party, on the point of departure for the tor, had heard the
dreadful tale she had to tell. Caradoc himself had heard
it some days later: how Cloudberry and the others had
followed the witch through the storm a little ahead of
Caradoc; how they had ascended through the darkness

to a hollow, close to the tor's summit; how the witch had vanished from their sight and then reappeared on the very highest rocky pinnacle, transformed, it seemed, into the likeness of a great black crow; how the bird had spread its huge wings against the pale light of the moss and risen above the pinnacle like some enormous primeval reptile; how the terrified Moorlanders had scattered in panic – Cloudberry back down the hill to safety and Dogberry to his death over the sheer precipice of the tor's eastern face. His screams had reached the ears of Caradoc on the slopes below the tor's summit. The rescue party had recovered his body the following day.

But before he heard of the fate of the unfortunate Dogberry, Caradoc had had his father to deal with. Here again the news had been mixed. Arken had been furious, of course, and his initial reaction was that Caradoc should be sent straight back to Buzzard Woods. But while he and his friends had been wandering blindly on the slopes of Vixen Tor, the Drizzlecombe Council had been in session and great decisions had been taken.

The council had resolved to send a patrol into the heart of the Wizard Lord's realm to achieve some purpose of Findhorn's which had been concealed from the majority of the council lest the Wizard Lord's spies, already reputed to be abroad, should hear of it. But the general populace had been entrusted with such knowledge as the council had of the layout of the Wizard Lord's castle. Its underground mines and dungeons were linked by a myriad of tunnels too small for the passage of men or even adult Moorlanders. The slaves of the Lord of the

Northmoor included children and young Simians who scampered to and fro along the tunnels carrying messages and materials between the larger shafts and chambers. Findhorn had declared it essential that the patrol should have access to those tunnels and he could think of no one better suited to the task than Caradoc. Fortinbras had nominated Ellie, or Fontanella as she was more formally known, to represent the Drizzlecombers in this role and, despite the initial objections of Arken, it had been decided that these two should accompany the patrol.

The patrol was to leave on the following day. Already the Simian warriors were wielding weaponry of a substance so firm and powerful that Moorlander swords could not prevail against them. As yet these arms were few and far between but the deeper the enemy delved the louder hummed his engines and the mightier grew his resources. Time was in his favour. Yet even now he had grown too strong for the Moorlanders to move against him openly. For whatever purpose Findhorn had in mind, he required only a picked few able to move quickly and silently up the river valleys into the heart of the Northmoor.

On the eve of their departure, the members of the patrol met in the great pound before Fortinbras' dome. A huge bonfire crackled against the evening sky and a great boar roasting on a spit drew the envy and admiration of the numerous onlookers peering in over the pound wall. Caradoc caught sight of a forlorn-looking Bluffinch straining to catch his attention. His first inclination was to ignore him but his better nature prevailed and he waved exuberantly in Bluffinch's direction. His friend's face lit up. Caradoc reflected on the irony of the fact that it was Bluffinch's much-vaunted physique that had denied him the glory of travelling north. He could not pass through the Wizard Lord's tunnels.

When Caradoc turned his attention from those gazing in upon the pound to those within it he was gripped with an initial sense of disappointment. There were so few of them. But as his gaze wandered, a shiver of excitement ran down his spine. This was some patrol! Arken and Hama were there in a huddle with Fortinbras and Narwhal. Caradoc was pleased to see Narwhal – although he did not know for what special skill he had been included. Polycanthus stood alongside, conversing with a tall female Grimspounder who Caradoc recognised as Lemuella, the champion archer. No doubt Polycanthus was invited for his fleet-footedness.

To their left a hearty fire burned noisily. Through its flames Caradoc espied the badgers – the huge intimidating bulk of Wolfsbane and two of his companions from the Blackdown Rings – and a fourth figure, dimly perceived through the flames but distinctly familiar. Caradoc suspected the heat of the fire was playing tricks on him. The fourth badger looked very like Hamilcar, but surely his friend was far away, safe in the valley of the Badgerbrook? He peered more intently, and, as he did so, the figure turned towards him and their eyes met. It was Hamilcar indeed and the faces of both lit up. This was not the time for emotional reunions but Caradoc could look forward to the time they would spend together on the journey north; perhaps Findhorn would teach them both the common tongue.

On the rear side of the fire at the head of the great feasting trestle sat Fontanella, who appeared to be involved in a heated argument with an enormous Drizzlecomber. As with the badgers, Caradoc had seen this face before. It belonged to Brand who had sat at table with himself and his father at the solstice feast. Caradoc was later to discover that Brand was Ellie's father. He would also discover that they were much given to argument with one another.

Enormous though Brand undoubtedly was, he was a mere sparrow when compared with the figure who sat alone at the opposite end of the trestle. Caradoc had hoped beyond hope that Bowerman would accompany them. The journey seemed far less dangerous in his company, and here he was.

This was the entire complement of the company, fourteen in all. No finer collection of brains and brawn could be assembled from amongst the enemies of the Wizard Lord.

That evening, all thoughts of the journey ahead were expunged from the minds of those soon to embark upon it. Even the sad and solitary Bowerman put aside his sorrows and came as close to dancing as was possible for a creature of his size. Entertainers of all descriptions – jugglers, magicians, acrobats and musicians – held the occupants of the pound enthralled until far into the night; and until far into the following day the company, intoxicated by their art, slumbered its last peaceful sleep for many a day.

The departure of the fourteen in mid-afternoon on the morrow was for Caradoc the most bittersweet of partings. His mother wept at the briefness of their meeting and the peril into which her son was now journeying. Almost a thousand Moorlanders lined the upper valley of the river and the company wound its way between vast columns of beaming, encouraging faces for what seemed an age. A number of younger Moorlanders, Bluffinch included, who publicly announced their disappointment at staying at home while secretly being glad of it, followed the company for some distance. But as the village slowly began to disappear from view, they gradually fell away until at last the fourteen were alone.

The plan was to follow the valley of the second river until it became lost in the great mires and then press on north and west over the high Southmoor towards the valley of the sixth river. Close to Combestone Tor, the sixth river split into two. The western arm flowed straight into the heart of the Northmoor and had its source hard upon the castle of their foe. By adopting this course, the company would spend as little time as possible exposed to danger on the open moor.

This much of the plan Caradoc knew. What they proposed to do when they reached their destination he had no idea but he was determined to find out. That evening, camp was struck in the wooded upper reaches of the river with the plateau of the Foxtor Mire providing some protection to the north and east. Caradoc, foiled in his designs to sit alongside Findhorn at table, was surprised and delighted that the Mage summoned both himself and Fontanella to attend him. Fontanella looked bored at the prospect. Caradoc, on the other hand, could not disguise his excitement.

"Are we going right up to his castle?" he blurted out immediately. "Won't he have lookouts?"

Findhorn smiled a smile with which Caradoc was becoming very familiar. "All in good time," he said. "Let's start at the beginning. Caradoc will remember the Solstice Council and the story I told of the rise of the Lord of the Northmoor – and of the creature he overthrew to achieve power. You, Ellie, are ignorant of the tale. But I think our inquisitive young friend here will recall every word of it and can enlighten you at his leisure." Caradoc glanced quickly at Ellie for any flicker of interest. Her expression was utterly neutral. He thought of the occasions too numerous to mention when he had endeavoured to appear intrigued by conversations which held no interest for him whatsoever. Whether the motivation for such pretences was embarrassment or just plain kindheartedness, Ellie obviously did not share it. Caradoc felt uncomfortable in case Findhorn should notice.

Findhorn continued unabashed. "It was originally thought that Magog did not survive his overthrow, that the deadly poison he consumed ended his life."

"Surely it must have done," Caradoc interjected. "Nothing can survive the white angel fungus – not even Magog."

"The Wizard Lord has many arts, some learnt from Magog and some not, some known to me but many, sadly, not. Somehow he has sustained life in his evil mentor for some unknown purpose of his own. Magog's mind, still keen, is imprisoned within his paralysed body and thus he has remained down the years. And down the years how

143

his malice, great to begin with, must have festered and grown. And how perfect and complete must be his thirst for revenge."

"So you want to wake him up so that the old wizard can kill the new?" said Ellie, cutting through Findhorn's rhetoric with devastating directness.

"Well… yes… That is indeed what I want."

"But how do you know he'll co-operate? Perhaps they'll join forces and then we'll have two of them to deal with."

There was sarcasm in her voice and Caradoc's sense of embarrassment became more intense.

"Perhaps I understand evil more than you do, my girl," snapped Findhorn, unable to disguise his irritation. "There cannot be two lords of the Northmoor. The advantage the good always have over the evil is that the good can work together. At best, the evil mistrust one another; at worst, there is mutual hatred. Magog will bend all his will to destroy the usurper. He may fail, of course, and be destroyed – they may even destroy one another – but his wrath will be terrible and it will not be turned against us, at least not at first. And if he is victorious we will not need to fear him for long. Our fungus expert, Potentilla of Sheepstor, has advised the council that the spores of the white angel will still be in his blood. We can only wake him for a while, not cure him. His ultimate fate will still be the same."

"Well, it still seems silly to me," persisted Ellie, seeming to relish antagonising the one person whom everyone else respected. "To seek to double the number of our enemies looks like madness."

"Well, what other choice do we have?" growled Findhorn, now becoming extremely irate. "We have no means to defeat him ourselves. We cannot overthrow him in battle. We cannot undermine him by subterfuge. There is only one power able to stand against him and that power we must utilise. It is our only hope."

This argument was delivered with such a sustained vigour that even Ellie was taken aback. She looked about to speak but hesitated, giving Findhorn the opportunity to continue uninterrupted.

"Anyway, whether you agree with me or not is irrelevant. The council has so decided. The only matter that concerns me is whether you are prepared to fulfill your allotted role in this undertaking. If you are then I shall explain the role to you. If you are not then we shall return to Drizzlecombe to find another to take your place. Are you willing to help?"

"I am," said Ellie quietly.

"I assume I do not need to ask you that question?" This time Findhorn's keen gaze fell upon Caradoc, who shook his head emphatically.

"Good. The main entrances to the castle will be heavily guarded. We will not even attempt to gain access there. But the Lord of the Northmoor was not the first to occupy this site. Magog dwelt there before him. And long before he arrived, races of men had lived and died there, and their castle of peat and stone still lies beneath the granite walls of the present pile. The remains of their dwellings are now a giant warren of tunnels, dungeons and mines running beneath the whole of the tor on which the castle is built. It is said that some branch out far into the surrounding moorland. Many are still used by the castle's master as connecting passages between his mines and dungeons. These are regularly maintained, wide and well used and must be avoided at all costs. Those that he does not use have fallen into disrepair, are narrow and in some cases blocked entirely. Adults, even adult Moorlanders, could not pass. That is where you will help. I now know the exact spot where the body of Magog is held, paralysed and imprisoned. I have plotted the route from a tunnel entrance remote from the castle and unguarded. Down this tunnel you will pass into the heart of the realm of the Wizard Lord and there you will awake the sleeping evil.

Caradoc gasped. Even Ellie winced visibly.

"Wake him? How? Won't he immediately destroy us?"

"No. I don't think he will," replied Findhorn, answering the last question first. "There is an antidote to the white angel fungus prepared for us by the skilled hands of Potentilla. It is only temporary, but it will restore him to full health for a while and you will administer it to him. It will not work immediately and thus you will have time to escape and let us into the Wizard Lord's dungeons by another way. You will have help, an expert digger, if the route becomes too narrow: your friend Hamilcar, Caradoc."

This was good news at least, for as well as an expert digger Hamilcar was also an extremely good fighter. Although Caradoc was bright enough to realise that if they did not reach the Sorcerer's body undetected, they would not reach it at all.

Caradoc glanced again at Ellie. All sign of emotions had vanished from her face. "Well, if that's all, I'll go," she said blankly.

"It is all," replied Findhorn. "Except that you will need this map of the dungeons – as far as we know them. Learn it well and quickly, for in two nights' time you will be inside them."

He handed her a folded paper and another to Caradoc and without looking at it she left.

After a safe time had elapsed, Caradoc enquired, "She is such an unpleasant girl. How could you possibly have chosen her as one of the company? I would rather have gone into the dungeons with Bluffinch."

"Yes, she is difficult," agreed Findhorn with a smile, "but she is courageous and resourceful. If I had been chosen to awaken the Sorcerer, I would have preferred her as a companion. Anyway Bluffinch is too big."

"How do you know all of this anyway and who made the map?" asked Caradoc, keen to make the best use of the time available by filling in the numerous gaps in his knowledge.

"I think that's about enough for this evening," Findhorn replied, still smiling. "I am tired if you're not. We will have ample time to talk on the journey tomorrow. Anyway you have your map to read."

They parted and Caradoc made his way back to his father's tent, trying in vain to pick out the detail of the map in the failing light. A column of burning brands had been erected in the circle of open space between the tents but a gusty wind had put many out and Caradoc could decipher nothing. Back in the tent, however, by the steady light of the beeswax candle he poured over every square inch of the map until, in the early hours, sleep overcame him.

He awoke on the morrow to an azure blue sky of brilliant sunshine. The wind of the previous evening had fallen away completely and the more seasoned travellers amongst them suspected that the journey over the high moor would be a hot and thirsty business. As the company picked its way slowly up the escarpment to the east of the riverbank, onto the central plateau of the Southmoor, Caradoc, as ever, sought out Findhorn. The Mage was unusually forthcoming. "There were many beings on the moor," he explained, "besides Moorlanders and men, who were working against the Wizard Lord." The great moorland buzzard hovered by day high over the Wizard Lord's fortress and brought to Findhorn news of its master's movements. By night, the silent tawny owl spied upon his works unseen. Some of Findhorn's creatures had even entered into the fortress itself. Some had not re-emerged but those who had, brought with them tales of a terrible captive held in the deepest dungeons, the very mention of whose name was punishable by instant death at the hands of the Wizard Lord himself.

"I only learnt of his survival a few days ago," Findhorn explained. "In fact on the day of our arrival in Drizzlecombe. Until then I had no real idea what we would do when we reached his realm – or even whether we should go there at all. This was a rival for our enemy indeed and one whose hatred for him would undoubtedly exceed his hatred for us."

Without prompting, Findhorn described the myriad of other creatures who played their part in the fight to save the moor. From the buzzards and badgers who harried the wandering bands of Simians all over the moor, to the humble and insignificant beasts who gnawed at the roots of the enemies' edifices, it seemed that all of nature was on their side.

"How can we possibly lose with so many against him?" asked Caradoc, flushed with excited optimism.

"We not only can lose, we are losing," retorted Findhorn. "So far I have only told you the good news. Most of it is wholly bad. He has already destroyed a vast area of the moor with his minings and workings, and his devastation multiplies with every day that passes. What he has destroyed will take generations to recover. You will see what I mean when we get there."

Caradoc's burst of enthusiasm was seriously dampened but Findhorn's unusually informative mood continued and Caradoc was soon engrossed in the Drizzlecombe legend of the Witch of Vixen Tor who lured travellers to their doom on the sheer precipices of the north face. Having experienced the wiles of the witch at first hand and lived to tell the tale, Caradoc felt as qualified to talk on the subject as Findhorn. There was one question he had to ask, however.

"The strangest thing was," he said, "that I would not have gone with her except that for a moment she looked just like my mother. And when she called me in the dark, it was my mother's voice."

"I do not know the answer to that for certain," replied

Findhorn disappointingly. "Perhaps you felt in danger at that time and thought of your mother." Caradoc was about to express scepticism at this explanation when Fontanella, who had quietly pulled alongside them during the course of the conversation, volunteered her own.

"Shapechanging," she declared bluntly. "She is a shapechanger."

"Hmph, I don't believe that either," said Caradoc, without really knowing what the word meant but feeling indignant that this brash youngster purported to know more than Findhorn.

Sensing that Caradoc was ignorant of the concept, Findhorn explained.

"Well, I don't know if I believe it either. But you never know, it might be true. It is said that there were shapechangers in the old days. Some were merely mages who had learnt the art of transforming themselves into the physical likenesses of animals. Others were more mysterious and strange, wandering spirits with no innate form, who could take upon themselves any shape they chose – even that of plants or inanimate objects. These were the true shapechangers. I myself have never seen or met one. If Vixana is a shapechanger she is the only one alive today – unless the Wizard Lord himself has learnt the art."

As the company plodded slowly onward across the sunny upland, the Mage's conversation drifted back into the even remoter past to the days when settlers first came to live upon the moor and when the common tongue began. All the questions Caradoc had planned to ask about the common tongue at a quieter moment were now answered. It was as if Findhorn wished to render him fluent in the common tongue there and then. If he wished to be a mage, Findhorn explained he would need to have access to all knowledge in whatever tongue it was to be found. Slowly Findhorn drifted forward through the ages, telling tales of mages ancient and modern whose life stories were an integral part of mage training. Caradoc listened intently to tales of Ferouak the Bold, who travelled to Armorica to slay a dragon and succeeded in dissuading the beast from continuing its depredations of the surrounding countryside and sending it peacefully on its way – the advantages of the common tongue again, Findhorn had said. He learnt also the story of Blanchard the Foolish, who allowed the secrets he had learnt to fall into the hands of strangers, who used them to bring about his downfall – the perils of an indiscriminate use of the common tongue, Caradoc thought, but did not say. Much lore Caradoc learnt in the course of this history and no part of it did he ever forget. The account ended with Findhorn's own father – the last great mage, Findhorn had said with unnecessary modesty.

Findhorn's tales occupied but a moment in Caradoc's consciousness but in reality they lasted a whole day. Caradoc did not stand with his fellows and gape in awe at the majestic torscape visible from the heights of the Southmoor – a great circle of peaks from Ryder in the South East through Haytor and Hameldown in the East to the great peaks of the Northmoor ahead of them. The panorama was immense. Caradoc thought nothing of it. Nor did he shiver at the lush green charms of Foxtor Mire only a few hundred yards to their east – the greatest bog on the moor. He did not swelter in the searing heat – the weather seemed wholly neutral to him – and when the company's course eventually brought it down off the high moor into the winding boulder-strewn valley of the western arm of the sixth river, he was wholly oblivious to the conflicting sense of relief at the coming shade and apprehension at the imminent peril felt by his companions. He was moved only by the words of the Mage. Only that evening did he wonder if Findhorn's sudden passion for dispensing knowledge might have some deeper motivation.

The company descended into the river valley in the late afternoon. The waters were full and rapid, for although no rain had fallen that day, that very same torrent which had deluged Caradoc and his friends at Vixen Tor still flowed in the moorland rivers. But this river was not like his own. A few trees lined its banks but it was not the shady woodland sanctuary of the rivers of home. Its waters were cool and clear, however, and the weary travellers dangled their tired feet in it for some while. Some two miles further northward the river rose onto the central fen of the Northmoor where it had its source. They were to make camp close to the foot of its ascent, for they must come upon the castle of their enemy on the morrow.

Their journey was quickly resumed therefore, and after a few more bends in the river, the hills on either side grew steeper and the last tree was left behind them. Dusk comes earlier in these steep-sided moorland valleys. While the high moor still bathed in sunshine, darkness came out of the river and quickly ran up the hillside. As they rounded the final bend, Polycanthus, at the end of the column, gave a cry of surprise.

"Hey, what's that along the river? Is it Simians?"

"Quiet, stupid," yelled Fortinbras with even greater volume, "and draw your weaponry."

"I don't think that will be necessary," said Findhorn calmly. "I think you'll find they are no threat."

Five hundred yards or so ahead of the east bank of the river was arrayed a host of twisted figures. They did indeed resemble Simians, or rather the sculptures of Simians in static pose, as if writhing in agony. As the company drew closer, the true nature of the cluster became apparent. The twisted shapes were trees – but the strangest trees that any of the company had ever seen. They seemed to grow from the mossy boulders on which they stood and the thin gnarled roots of each tree enveloped its granite base like ivy stems around an oak. They grew no higher than the head of a tall Moorlander; Bowerman could see over the whole wood. The icy winds howling down off the high moor had stunted their growth and their desperate attempts to avoid its blast had sculpted their agonised demeanour. There was an air of menace about the place and the whole company felt uneasy.

"Is this the work of our foe?" asked Polycanthus.

"No, it is the work of the moor," replied Findhorn. "Woods do not normally grow in such places."

Caradoc, for one, was not reassured. He surveyed the surrounding hills. Due north he looked upon the forbidding prospect of Crow Tor, its huge granite peak resembling an enormous bird of prey leaning threateningly towards them. It reminded him strangely of the entranced meditations of the witch.

"I do not like this place," he said quietly to his father.

"Nor do I," replied Arken, "and yet I fear there are worse places to come." He immediately regretted his words for fear of alarming his son unnecessarily.

Campfires were rapidly kindled and tents quickly erected on the riverbank due south of the wood. Light was now failing fast and Caradoc decided to briefly explore the groves of the ancient wood before darkness fell completely. Findhorn had assured him that the wood itself was not evil. He would keep within sight of the campfires and he only need jump to catch a glimpse of the camp over the treetops. He picked his way carefully into the wood, making sure he did not turn his ankle in the crevices between the rocks. Other than the moss and the trees, very little else seemed to grow in the wood. He fancied he glimpsed the wing of a pale bird amidst the distant branches but other than that the whole forest seemed dead. Even the trees seemed more dead than alive.

The physical effort of climbing over boulders forced him slowly downhill towards the riverbank. Soon the woodland began to thin and in the clear moonlight he glimpsed the silver of the waters through the trees. He had reached the last ten yards or so of woodland when he froze and slipped behind the closest tree. He grasped the trunk with both hands and peered around it towards the river. At the water's edge a black animal, the size of a large dog, was drinking. He could not pick out its features as its head was thrust below the curve of the riverbank but there was something about its stance that suggested carnivore. And then into the moonlight walked a man. He appeared to have emerged from the woodland not far from the north of Caradoc's tree and he strode confidently across the grass towards the drinking creature. The figure was tall and slim and appeared to be that of a young man. He bore no weapon that Caradoc could see. The features of the man's face were obscured, as the back and sides of his head were entirely enclosed within a strange metal helmet which followed exactly the contours of his head and cascaded over his shoulders. If it truly was made of metal, Caradoc thought, what wonderful protection it must be. As the man drew nearer to the drinking creature he whistled a shrill piercing sound that brought Caradoc's hands involuntarily to his ears. Immediately the creature turned. Its jaw was huge, square and canine, and river water gushed from between the parted teeth. Its eyes were red and wild, and Caradoc felt sure it was about to spring upon the defenceless man.

But it did nothing of the sort. Its attitude was entirely submissive. It whimpered and advanced meekly in answer to the summons. The man turned back towards the woods and the hound followed. Caradoc now glimpsed the man's face for the first time. It was as old and sere as the body was young and fit. The skin was ashen grey and wrinkled like a hedgehog's but the eyes burned with a keen fire – a fire that Caradoc felt he had seen somewhere before. Such an intelligence flickered in its glow that Caradoc shrank back behind the trunk in an irrational fear of detection; he remembered Hama's story of the Simian on Saddlemoor Down. If the man possessed the Simian powers of perception, however, they obviously did not work in this strange primeval wood, and master and hound disappeared into the woodland.

Caradoc remained pressed motionless against the tree for some minutes in case the stranger should lead his animal in his direction. As soon as he was convinced that the coast was clear he released his grasp on the gnarled trunk and slipped away back into the wood towards the camp. He had travelled only a few yards when a great din of rushing and clanking brought him to a halt. He again slipped behind the nearest tree trunk and looked back just in time to see a sleek black chariot explode at great speed from amongst the groves and rocket away to the north. Other than its unusual sleekness and the opulent nature of the metalwork bedecking its sides, there was nothing particularly strange about the vehicle itself. It was the creatures that drew it that caused Caradoc to gape in stunned amazement. Instead of the moorland ponies which drew the rickety Moorlander chariots, or the horses which drew the more substantial vehicles of the men of the East, this sinister conveyance was hauled by the black hound and three other equally enormous colleagues. The only passenger was the wrinkled stranger who, tall and imperious at the helm of the chariot, directed their course with a series of shrill whistles like some despotic shepherd.

The pulling power of the pack was plainly considerable, for the chariot receded into the distance with great rapidity and within a minute or so it had vanished. Caradoc disappeared through the woodland in the opposite direction with equal speed, desperate to report this new sighting to Findhorn and the rest of the company.

CHAPTER FIFTEEN

THE POISONED LAND

By mid-morning on the morrow, the company had left the northern edge of the ancient wood behind them and commenced the ascent onto the great northern fen past the massif of Bear Down through a pass to the east of Crow Tor. Caradoc rode alone to the rear and pondered on the events of the previous night and the reactions of two of the company to his story.

He had hoped that Findhorn might immediately reveal the identity of this master of hounds, perhaps even enlist him on their side. But Findhorn could cast very little light on the mystery. Caradoc had suggested that he might be some wandering leader of the Easterners but Findhorn had doubted it. Few men, however powerful, wandered of their own accord alone onto the Northmoor in these dangerous times, he had said.

Bowerman, who had said very little to anyone since the company had left Drizzlecombe, had displayed an intense interest in Caradoc's account and had quizzed him for some time after the rest of the company had retired. Afterwards, Caradoc had noticed him standing alone on the river's edge staring distractedly northwards. Caradoc had hidden behind a waterside rock and watched him. The sad, dark eyes beneath the heavy brows spoke of some private grief which Caradoc's story had perhaps rekindled. He was seized with a sense of great shame at intruding upon it and slipped away back to his tent.

As they progressed, the path became steeper and the terrain more difficult; Caradoc dismounted and led the tired Neb behind him. Dreaming as always, he began to fall behind the rest of the group. His musings were distracted by the sound of rocks falling from the slopes above him. He glanced upwards in time to see a dark shape disappear behind the rockfall. The glance was so fleeting that for a moment Caradoc wondered whether he was still dreaming. He considered calling ahead for assistance but refrained from doing so for fear of appearing foolish should the peril prove imaginary. A moment's pause satisfied him that there was no danger and he jogged on after his friends, pulling Neb briskly along behind him. He had gone no more than ten yards when the shape behind the rock, or one very like it, materialised on the slopes before him, a shape now familiar to Caradoc, with the same idiotic monkey grin that haunted his waking dreams.

159

The monkey drew its short sword and waited for his small foe to cower.

But Caradoc no longer feared the Simians; he had seen them overcome and was prepared to try himself. He drew his own blade and advanced but as he did so a second monkey leapt from a nearby boulder and planted itself alongside his fellow. The odds were now unfavourable and Caradoc hollered as loudly as he was able for help. But within a second, the odds had altered dramatically and his respect for the martial skills of the warlike Wolfsbane had increased tenfold. The second Simian advanced towards him, brandishing its spiked mace with every intention of caving in his skull. A glint of light flashed to the left of its head. And in the blink of an eye, the Simian's head was no longer attached to its shoulders but bouncing away down the hill into the river valley, taking giant leaps each time it struck a boulder. Wolfsbane stepped from behind a rock, brandishing his enormous axe.

The first Simian now realised its plight, especially as other members of the company now appeared behind it. But within a moment it was joined by a third and the two survivors prepared for a valiant last-ditch defence. Simians were despicable but they were not all cowardly and momentarily Caradoc felt a bit sorry for them. But he realised the company could have no room for pity at such a time; soon the odds would be dramatically reversed and any steps they could take now to redress the balance should be taken. This, Findhorn later told him, was one of the greatest evils perpetrated by any despot: the fact that others were reduced to behaving as he.

Two arrows flew from the bows of Bowerman and Lemuella, and the Simians fell dead. There was more work to do, however – and quickly too. For as most of the company knew by now, Simians travelled in foursomes. Fortinbras organised the company in groups of two and sent them out to scour the hillside. It was imperative that the remaining Simian did not escape to bring news of their approach to his master. The search did not last long. Wolfsbane again was the executioner. He returned, flourishing the severed head, and Caradoc was shocked to see that it still bore the stock Simian grin.

The company reassembled and pressed onwards, keeping all the time to the east bank of the river. As they rose onto the high moor, the last remaining vegetative cover disappeared. Other than the numerous isolated granite piles they were now crossing completely open moorland. The company now crossed the Wildbanks, a high ridge of land not far from the river's source. From here they would descend into the depression of Cowflop Bottom, which joined the east and west arms of the sixth river. They would follow this depression to the eastern arm which followed a path, peculiarly straight for a moorland river, to the slopes below the Wizard Lord's castle.

Findhorn now sought out his young pupil and as they rose onto the Wildbanks he endeavoured to give him his first halting instruction in the common tongue. He explained how the variations of meaning based upon the duration, rhythm and cadence did not vary from species to species but that those based on pitch and tone varied to suit the vocal character of each – only gentle and subtle variations, he explained, rather like those of dialect. He then instructed Caradoc in the names of the various creatures of the moor. Caradoc had encountered no difficulty in absorbing the ancient tales of the previous day but this was neither the place nor the time for him to cope with the complexities of a new language. He did his best but Findhorn soon became impatient of his errors, which only served to confuse him even further. Findhorn pressed on regardless, as if the knowledge might soon be lost and had to be shared immediately.

As the company reached the ridge of the Wildbanks, the Great Northern Fen loomed into view from the north. Even Findhorn stood transfixed. The fen was the heart of the moor – not its geographical centre, that was a little way to the south and east, but the very essence of the moor. It was a great sponge, a vast blanket bog that absorbed all the rains that came out of the western seas and from which sprang most of the moorland's rivers. From the hinterland of Cut Hill it stretched out far to the north and west, a place of wild beauty and exhilarating desolation. Around its edge, the fen was encircled by an array of the greatest tors of the moor. Great Mis to the south and Great Links to the west; to the north the two giant tors of Yes and High Willhayes; and to the east, and visible for the first time now, the peak of Hangingstone Hill, below which their enemy had made his fortress. No sound came from the wilderness except the plaintive piping of the curlew drifting across the waving sedge grass. But many creatures dwelt there. Buzzards, merlins, harriers and kestrels hovered over the bogs, advertising by their presence the existence of a myriad of tiny creatures, denizens of the bog itself. Larger creatures such as badgers and deer had learnt its safeways. But neither mankind nor Moorlander lived upon the fen nor had they ever done so.

For some while they lingered on the ridge, drinking in the solitude of the land spread out before them. It crossed the mind of not a few of them that even this pristine wilderness might not escape the desecrations of the Wizard Lord. Full of such deeply pessimistic thoughts the company moved off slowly from the ridge into the channel of Cowflop Bottom, making for the eastern river.

The distance was not great and by early afternoon the line of the river was in sight. As they approached the water Caradoc noticed that some of the more advanced members of the company had covered their faces with their cloaks. Within a few paces he learnt the cause. A foul stench like the carcass of some rotting beast hung heavily in the air, and his eyes began to tingle and then smart. Carcasses of deer or other ungulates were a relatively common occurrence on the moor, particularly after harsh winters, and Caradoc always winced at the sight and gave them a wide berth. They were continuing reminders of the creatures' suffering. But there were none to be seen; the reek obviously had another source. Its nature soon became apparent.

The company stood upon the bank and gazed at the water. But this was not the pure silver elixir in which they had cooled their tired feet the previous evening. They would not have immersed their feet in this, even to escape the hordes of the Wizard Lord. Between the banks flowed, where it moved at all, a liquid of the dullest orange. On the surface thick off-white suds surrounded little islands of congealed encrusted scum. The whole noxious brew bubbled spasmodically and stank continuously.

"What evil is this?" Caradoc heard a voice positively growl. He glanced to his left and immediately stepped back in alarm. The usually melancholy features of Bowerman were contorted into a wild rage. "Will he never be content? Why must he destroy that which he seeks to rule?" he snarled.

"Because only by doing so can he find the means to rule it," ventured Findhorn.

"Then he must be stopped… at any cost."

Bowerman cast his eyes northward. There was resolution in his voice – a new resolution. Slowly his features relaxed back to their accustomed pensiveness. He added almost as an afterthought, "There is little enough of the old world left."

As the company proceeded, a safe distance from the polluted river, up the valley towards the distant Whitehorse Hill, Caradoc pondered on the strange transformation of his feelings for the great warrior. At first he had viewed him with a sense of awe and no little fear. This was the world's most formidable pugilist and only a fool would cross him. But now whenever he thought of Bowerman he felt only sadness and pity. Bowerman appeared a lonely figure, awkward in the company of others and confused by the ways of a world he did not seem to understand. He was the last of an ancient breed and Caradoc wondered whether this contribution to the affairs of the modern world might be his last.

Caradoc spent the rest of the afternoon's journey in the company of his father and Narwhal, and together they reminisced on happier times in their respective marks. Even Ellie joined in the conversation, relating a jolly little tale concerning Lungwort and a spectral pig, its otherworldliness enhanced by a liberal dousing of marsh phosphorous applied by Cloudberry and Dogberry. Caradoc was amused by the tale and impressed by Ellie's rendition of it but his enjoyment was tempered by his recollection of the events at Vixen Tor and the fate of Dogberry.

Findhorn remained alone but lost in his own thoughts, his earlier enthusiasm for instruction entirely gone. All attempts by Caradoc to make conversation with him were met by a bluff rebuttal.

At about teatime, the company crossed a ford only a mile or so from the head of the river and made eastwards for the foot of Whitehorse Hill. Findhorn's map revealed the existence of a cavern on the northern edge of the hill, which appeared to offer a good vantage point for viewing events on the opposite side of the valley – assuming of course that they could reach it undetected. It was resolved after much deliberation to delay the final push around the Western edge of the tor until after nightfall and the company settled down in an obscure hollow to wait for darkness.

Two hours later the light had almost failed entirely and a spectacular sunset had long since been swallowed up by the western bogs. A number of the group were still in the latter stages of a well-earned slumber but amongst the wakeful there was a growing hubbub of activity as preparations were made to leave. Caradoc peered over the edge of the hollow across the darkling heather and as he did so, he heard a familiar sound. Distant but distinct, a buzzard mewed high above the tor. The cry was the sound of the woods of home. Findhorn immediately sprang to his feet.

"At last, she's here," he exclaimed excitedly and nipped with surprising agility over the rim of the coombe towards the hill. The bird wheeled eastwards towards them and descended gracefully and effortlessly with hardly a motion of its wings. Caradoc made as to follow Findhorn but a glance stopped him in his tracks. This was not a council at which he was welcome.

The buzzard alighted on a thistle bush some forty or so yards away. Caradoc could dimly make out the form of a large female. Her white bib and large proud eyes glinted in the faint light. The grey outline of Findhorn squatted beside her. Caradoc strained his ears in the vain hope of picking up something of the exchange. He fancied he heard a thin whistle rising and falling on the breeze, but perhaps it was the wind itself. At any rate it made no sense to him.

Within minutes, the bird had risen again upon the column of air and banked away to the north. Findhorn had returned to camp and was busily organising the departure. As the company surrendered up the safety of the hollow, Caradoc wondered how they would negotiate the difficult contours of the tor in total darkness. He had no cause to worry, however, for as the last of the campfires were extinguished a new light flickered in the hand of Findhorn. The secret of the osmundacea moss was known to others than the Witch of Vixen Tor – and Findhorn was among them. But the glow of the moss alone would not see them safely through the dark. Help from another source was required – and it arrived quickly. As if summoned by the glow, the thin but reassuring whistle of the buzzard sounded faintly from somewhere high above them. As far as Caradoc was concerned the sound could have come from anywhere but Findhorn could plainly locate it exactly and immediately set off to the west. The uneven softness of the ground initially suggested that he might have got it all wrong but after a few minutes the going became more easy and before long they were walking on trackway – ancient and overgrown but a discernible route nevertheless. Every so often the bird mewed and their direction changed, but always they kept to the pathway, a track laid down centuries before by a race of men who had made their homes upon these hills before conflict came out of the East. The track was long disused but its makers had also drawn the map in Findhorn's possession and its course led them straight to the cave which by day gazed directly down upon the evil workings of their enemy.

CHAPTER SIXTEEN

THE LAWS OF HUNTING

The cave did not make comfortable lodgings and most of the company were longing for daybreak, many hours before it came. Findhorn had given strict instructions that no one was to emerge from the cave before the return of Windhover the Buzzard, as it was not known how exposed their bolthole was to prying eyes from across the valley or how many Simian scouts might prowl their own hill. They did not have long to wait. The bird arrived with the dawn, alighting at the cave's entrance noisily and ostentatiously in apparent disregard of the Simian threat. Findhorn emerged, blinking, into the sunlight to greet her and having spent a minute or so in absorbing the news she brought, invited the others out to join him. As Caradoc followed Hamilcar onto the narrow ledge, a low growl from the badger's throat warned him of the spectacle awaiting him. He did not, however, anticipate the total horror of the scene that lay before him.

The Wizard Lord's hill lay due north of the tor on which they stood. Between the peaks lay a high valley some 400 yards or so across. Caradoc's gaze first fell upon the random heaps of waste and slime strewn across the valley. The bases of the piles were in most cases white or a dirty off white, but the conical peaks sported a variety of vivid colours, from rich red copper to lime green. The rivulets of colour trickled down the hillsides and accumulated in thick steaming pools at the bottom. From above, the piles of slag resembled little eruptions from some enormous subterranean septic tank. An all-pervading stench hovered over the valley reminiscent of that which had assailed the company at Cowflop Bottom.

Caradoc's gaze drifted beyond the slag piles to the tor beyond; a huge pall of greeny smoke formed a dismal shroud enveloping the tor's lower slopes, but even as they looked a compliant breeze blew down off the western plateau and parted the cloud, revealing the Wizard Lord's seat of power.

Caradoc was extremely disappointed. He had expected a forbidding and sinister castle complete with drawbridge, arrow-slits and bleak, high turrets. The edifice that presented itself through the smog was appropriately huge, there could be no doubt about that. But it was not remotely exciting. Indeed the predominant impression was one of bland uniformity. The massive unadorned walls rose from the granite of the tor itself. Their substance was entirely formed by a smooth pale stone without a single interruption or blemish – not even for the admission of light. This was perhaps not surprising; the valley did not present a pleasant aspect and despite the enthusiasm with which their enemy created such noxious fumes, he presumably did not relish the prospect of their drifting around his living quarters. The immense monotony of the building and the regularity and severity of its angles was intimidating, and Caradoc could not see how on earth they would enter it.

More terrifying still were the distant cries of the tiny figures scurrying like busy insects across the valley floor. Caradoc could not see but strongly suspected that many were Moorlanders. He also could not see by what means their captives compelled their co-operation but he had heard tales of their ferocious hogweed whips and he shuddered at the thought.

There was silence for some minutes. Then Findhorn spoke.

"Behind those ramparts is the power we must overthrow and somehow we must enter in. He may not know we are here yet but he will soon learn and so we must act quickly." Findhorn then explained his plan, that which he had disclosed to Caradoc and Fontanella on the first night of their journey. He described the route the party would take as scouted by Windhover the Buzzard. But who should accompany Caradoc and Ellie, and what should they do once their object was achieved? Their discussions were long and heated but by mid-afternoon the company was in agreement and those who were to undertake the task settled down to sleep before the perilous journey ahead.

Within a dimly lit hall deep in the heart of a mountain fastness, two columns of soldiers stood silently in the half-light. A long narrow trough separated the two columns and from it sprang flames of a perfect whiteness fired by some unseen source. The soldiers were mostly Simians but a few were men, who seemed by some strange means to have acquired the stooping Simian gait. Each wore the masked helmet of the Simian and carried their familiar curved sabre at his waist. At the far end of the hall three steps led up to a raised dais on which rested an enormous granite throne. The throne was empty but in the shadows behind it lurked the even darker shadow of an immense creature. Many among the silent soldiers knew its nature but to those who did not, it appeared as a biped like themselves but of immeasurably greater height and girth. And they quaked in terror not knowing what would befall them.

At the foot of the steps knelt two small figures, hooded and bound. What these creatures were and the reason for their presence was not apparent, but there could be no doubt that they had greater cause for fear than those who stood in safe anonymity in their columns.

An age seemed to pass without sound and without any discernible movement but at last to the rear of the throne a thick brown bearskin curtain parted and a single figure

171

appeared. Alongside the guardian of the throne, the figure seemed slight but it strode confidently forward to the front of the dais and gazed down upon the assembled throng. As it did so, all heads bowed. Then it spoke, in a clear, high-pitched, androgynous voice.

"Well, first of all we must deal with our little helpmates," the voice sneered. "Have your friends found me enough goodies or have they not, do you think? Have they valued your lives highly enough to give me a fair day's work for a fair day's pay or have they applied themselves so little that I am unable to afford the pleasure of your company for even a moment longer?"

As he said this, he smiled demurely in the direction of the guardian of the throne. The shadow stepped forward. It was the giant Simian of the Grimspound raid and it wielded an immense mace. The bound figures prepared for oblivion.

"Well, it is your lucky day, your friends have worked hard. Your skulls will remain intact – for this week. Take them away." The bound figures were ushered quickly from the hall.

"We have more important matters to consider than executions, exquisite though they may be. For there are more of the little people coming to join us. And they are bringing some bigger friends with them – one very big one, one of yours in fact." He gesticulated dismissively towards the giant Simian. Whether the creature was moved by this intelligence could not be discerned for it had resumed its place in the shadows behind the throne. Its master continued.

"Why are they coming? The free-dwellers of the moor do not normally visit their northern neighbour unsolicited. This I do not know and this you will very soon tell me – or there will be fewer of you."

The transformation in the speaker's demeanour during this tirade was complete. Gone was the self-satisfied sarcasm, replaced by the purest and profoundest rage, rage at the democratic arrogance of the free-dwellers. Now was the terror of his slaves at its greatest; he was capable of anything now. For minutes he uttered no words. Only a low steady gurgling from the throat of the Wizard Lord broke the silence. Then, with a gesticulated summons to the Simian lieutenants at the head of each column to follow him, he vanished behind the bearskin curtain.

One mile distant, Caradoc sat cross-legged atop a granite slab. On a long, low kistvaen beside the slab rested the snout of Hamilcar, less pronounced than that of Wolfsbane but a fine figure of a snout nevertheless. Caradoc had tried to indicate to him that it was disrespectful to rest his snout on gravestones, even if they were only the graves of men, but one day was not enough to learn the common tongue. The clear, contrasting markings of the offending snout stood out distinctly in the bright moonlight and Caradoc began to feel a little exposed on his rocky seat. He slipped quietly down alongside Bowerman who was resting with his broad back against the cool granite. Ellie sat silently beside him.

The group whispered quietly to one another, awaiting

the return of the buzzard. The bird had flown on ahead to scout the route. In the absolute stillness of the evening, even the gentlest whisper seemed a din. The conversation soon subsided, and Bowerman and Ellie passed the time by studying the detail of Findhorn's map.

Caradoc, however, already knew the map intimately. He preferred to study the great map in the sky. He stretched out flat upon the ground, his hands behind his head, and scrutinised the pale perfect orb high above him. Despite the brightness of the night, the sky was not entirely clear. From time to time little wisps of blue-grey cloud drifted out from total darkness across the moon's face and back into total darkness. He studied the distant contours and wondered whether any of them represented a great moorland plateau with little rivers like his own and whether, like his own, a soulless destroyer threatened its very existence.

With his thoughts soaring through the heavens, Caradoc did not at first notice a rustling in the gorse bushes away beyond the kistvaen. Then a snorting and a grunting were added to the rustling and even the dreaming Caradoc became alarmed. Hamilcar bared his fangs silently, and Ellie and Caradoc carefully unsheathed their swords. If the Simians had found them so soon they would pay dearly for their efficiency. Bowerman, on the other hand, made no pugilistic preparations whatsoever. Evidently he knew something the others did not. The cacophony drew closer and they could now plainly make out a busy systematic sniffing.

As Bowerman smiled, the cause of the din appeared.

Caring nothing for the perils of the moorland night, a large hedgehog trotted into view. It glanced casually in the direction of Hamilcar, disregarded his companions entirely and then careered off at a right angle to noisily explore an interesting hollow where it began to dig furiously, snorting vigorously all the while.

Ellie fixed her eyes on Bowerman's bow.

"Come on, Bowerman, put an arrow in it, it'll bring every Simian for miles around down on us."

"I shall do nothing of the sort," bellowed Bowerman at a volume which almost drowned out the hedgehog's noisy foraging.

"Why not? You're supposed to be the Hunter," continued Ellie unabashed.

Caradoc stared at her dumbfounded. She never ceased to amaze him; he felt admiration for her boldness, embarrassment at her insolence and disgust at her callousness.

"It is precisely because I am a hunter that I will not take the life of this creature," retorted Bowerman. "I am called the Hunter because I have lived as a hunter. I have not lived by growing crops or tending sheep. I have lived as the wolf and the eagle. I have killed for my living but I have obeyed the ancient laws of hunting and have killed only when I needed to do so. No animal, saving only man – and some Moorlanders it seems – does otherwise. To kill any living creature, plant or animal, needlessly or for pleasure is the essence of evil. Indeed, to take pleasure from killing, even when you find the need, is reprehensible and the ancient law decrees that anyone who does must cease to be a hunter and take up some other occupation. All life, ourselves included, comes from the Goddess and returns to it. Therefore to take the life of one of her creatures wantonly is to diminish yourself. To encourage me to do so is to do the work of the creature we seek to overthrow. Perhaps he has other weapons than his Simians."

This was an oration worthy of Findhorn; and it was even more persuasive coming from the usually taciturn Bowerman who now seemed quite exhausted by the effort. The effect on Ellie was more difficult to gauge. She was certainly shocked, for she had no spontaneous retort. But the expression on her face still bore a glint of defiance and Caradoc suspected that she would still like to shoot the hedgehog. Wisely it had continued its journey on into the night and its grunts were still audible some distance away. A large cloud had obscured the moon and conferred upon the creature the blessing of total darkness. It would never know the moral controversies its innocent foraging had inspired. Caradoc wondered whether its intended insect victims were protected by the ancient laws of hunting.

CHAPTER SEVENTEEN

THE HOUSE OF THE WIZARD LORD

Another hunter, Windhover the Buzzard, returned as the moon vanished, rushing from the north. Their wait was now over. The path ahead was clear for the moment and the final leg of their journey to the mouth of the concealed tunnel revealed by Findhorn's map must be undertaken immediately. Findhorn took Caradoc aside and passed him a slim glass phial containing a catmint green liquid.

"You remember what to do with this?" he asked.

"Of course," Caradoc replied. Findhorn did not doubt it.

"But it looks so flimsy. Won't it smash?"

"The contents are a Moorlander creation, by your

clever Potentilla, your mother's teacher in the herbal arts. But the phial is mine. Even Bowerman couldn't break it. Just don't lose it."

"I won't," said Caradoc. He placed it in a secure inner pocket of his jacket but knew he would never stop checking that it was still there.

Caradoc and Arken embraced. There were no further words to be said between them. Arken had agonised as to whether to let him go. He knew that if their quest failed, Caradoc, like every other Moorlander, might have no future and he accepted Findhorn's view that Caradoc was the best person for the job. He wondered if Imogen would agree with him. But it was too late now for second thoughts; their embrace ended and the group were gone.

Unbeknown to Caradoc and his companions, a force of Simians, one hundred strong, was issuing at that very moment from the main gate of the fortress. Counting upon a frontal assault, their master had resolved to meet it head on. At the head of the force he placed his greatest warrior, the giant Simian; and as Findhorn looked down upon the enemy's hordes from his mountain bolthole, the Lord of the Northmoor reclined in his throne room awaiting news of the slaughter, never guessing that miles to the east a little band of adventurers was preparing to strike at him from the heart of his own kingdom.

The bird having rested, the party set off in its wake. The dark bulk of the hill loomed up forbiddingly some distance away to their left. The immediate surroundings of the tor were submerged beneath a thick forest of dark green heather which obscured somewhere in its depths the long-forgotten portal of an ancient race, by which they hoped to enter. The heather would also provide admirable cover and they made for it as quickly as the darkness and the difficult terrain would allow.

To Caradoc's surprise he was joined by an uncharacteristically talkative Ellie, plainly still smarting from the rebuke of Bowerman.

"His stupid laws of hunting could have done for all of us. He risked every single creature on the moor for one hedgehog. I think even your old wizard would have had something to say about that."

"Perhaps he would say that as soon as we begin to behave like the enemy we are all done for anyway."

"But we aren't behaving like him. He kills for pleasure. We will never do that. But we shouldn't give him an unfair advantage by fighting him with our hands tied behind our back. We must do whatever is necessary to defeat him. I don't think the badger would have been so squeamish. Perhaps we should have brought him after all!"

She was referring to the heated deliberations that had taken place about who should accompany them. Caradoc and Ellie were essential, of course, as theirs was to be the task of navigating endless subterranean tunnels down which the adults could not pass. Hamilcar had no equal as a digger – and he was the smallest of the badgers. But who was to protect them? It had been accepted by all that no more than one or two could accompany them, as freedom from detection was far more important than martial prowess. Arken had been keen to watch over his son. Brand, similarly motivated by paternal considerations, had also wished to be included. But both had been forced to concede that there was only really one choice: no one could repel Simian onslaughts quite like Bowerman. And so all were agreed – all except one. Wolfsbane thought he could do the job just as well; and what was more, he claimed, he would be less conspicuous on the open eastern trackways than would the enormous Bowerman. Ellie had rather unkindly pointed out that great noise was just as likely to attract attention as great size. It had been left to Findhorn to persuade him more gently that his talents would be better utilised elsewhere.

Some two hours after the confrontation with the hedgehog, the party plunged into the outer fringes of the heather jungle concealing the ancient mineworks. Heavy fronds slapped their faces as they passed beneath the giant plants. Now more than ever were they thankful for the nugget of osmundacea moss entrusted to Caradoc by Findhorn; they would have even greater need of it in the pitch blackness of the Wizard Lord's dungeons.

The path through the heather was not long but it was uncomfortable and difficult. Windhover the Buzzard, his task completed, had departed southwards and the scramble through the undergrowth was led by Hamilcar whose powerful forepaws forged a path through which even Bowerman could pass. The wetness of the turf was easy upon hands and knees but the faces of the travellers were soon caked in brown mud, until Caradoc began to wonder whether the Simians would even recognise them as Moorlanders. He even fancied he caught sight of Ellie giggling at him in an unguarded moment, although he doubted whether he looked any sillier than she did.

The sheer slopes of the tor brought their suffering to an abrupt halt. Between the heather forest and the tor itself, a convenient ribbon of mossy sward encircled the hill's eastern face and for some minutes the tired travellers lay prostrate upon it in the moonlight. Their strength regained, they huddled around the old map, hoping to pinpoint the exact door through which the ancient moormen had dragged their hard-won treasures into the sunlight an age ago. Whether the riches they sought were those now coveted by his enemy, Caradoc did not know. The old tales told of their desire to dominate other men but they did not speak of a cruel or vengeful people; in those vices the modern lords of the Northmoor reigned supreme.

Faults the ancient moormen may have had but mapmaking was not among them and they quickly located the tunnel entrance. It seemed only a few paces away. Locating it on the ground, however, proved more difficult than finding it on the map. Bowerman and Hamilcar scythed their way through an ocean of brambles and the short June night had nearly run its course when at last Bowerman's blade struck metal with a harsh clang, and the faded timbers and rusted clasps of a once mighty gate were laid bare. As Bowerman set his mind to the best means of forcing access without bringing every Simian in the vicinity down upon them, Caradoc and Ellie curled up on the soft undergrowth to snatch a few hours' well-earned rest.

Caradoc awoke with the first glimpse of dawn. It seemed that he had slept for but a moment and yet he felt strong and refreshed. Ellie still slept peacefully. A few feet away from her, Hamilcar was laid stretched out on his belly. His paws covered his snout as if to muffle the prodigious snoring that emanated therefrom. If that was his intention he was failing abysmally; so much for the silent patrol, thought Caradoc.

He looked beyond the sleeping figures towards the eastern torscape. The rim of the rising sun was creeping over the edge of the eastern escarpment as if it was having difficulty in summoning up the effort to make the final ascent. The liquid light expanded in both directions like a distant mountain sea. Its colour seemed strange; perhaps the Lord of the Northmoor had corrupted even the light of the sun. And that was not all that was strange. In the valley of Buzzard Woods the birds serenaded the rising sun. But in the heart of the Northmoor the coming of the light aroused no comment. The moorland dawn rang with a deafening silence. There were no birds to greet the dawn; but for the occasional foolhardy hedgehog, the land was empty. For the first time since he had left Drizzlecombe, Caradoc felt genuinely afraid; he did not want to enter the tunnel.

As Caradoc surveyed the horizon he became aware of a figure in the foreground. Bowerman sat silently upon a rock observing him.

"Beautiful, isn't it?" he exclaimed. "I've watched it for almost an hour."

"I wonder if the Lord of the Northmoor is admiring it at this very moment," Caradoc mused.

"I doubt it very much," said Bowerman. "I don't think he admires anything that is not his own creation."

Bowerman fell silent, staring directly into the sunlight.

"What are you thinking?" ventured Caradoc softly.

"I am wondering whether somewhere – anywhere – in the world the sun is rising upon one of my people."

"What do you mean?" asked Caradoc. "It must be."

"Only if somewhere in the world, one of my people still lives."

Bowerman spoke so quietly that Caradoc had difficulty in understanding him. He scrutinised his friend closely. Bowerman's eyes, melancholic at the best of times, now seemed utterly forlorn. Surely he could not be the only Giganticus alive. How lonely he must be if he were. Caradoc did not like to ask.

The awkward silence was broken by a torrent of uncontrolled snorts. Ellie immediately sat bolt upright and gazed around her in alarm.

"Are we being attacked?" she exclaimed.

"Attacked?" chuckled Caradoc. "It was only Hamilcar waking up."

Ellie scowled at the badger and set about her kitbag with a venom entirely wasted on inanimate objects. Bowerman and Caradoc embarked upon the same task with a little more composure, and Caradoc took the opportunity to pose the question he had avoided earlier.

"But there must be others. The Goddess would not allow your people to die out."

"Ah... the Goddess. She allows many things... the Lord of the Northmoor, for example, and the Witch of

Vixen Tor. But then is the witch not a goddess herself within her own little land and is not our enemy a god in his?"

"No, of course they're not," snapped Caradoc indignantly. "There is only one Goddess of everything and everywhere."

"That is what you Moorlanders believe but in the days when Gigantici roamed freely in the southern lands they found a goddess in every grove and a god in every river. Every manifestation of nature had its own proper spirit and the woods rang with their distant laughter and the rivers ran to their sweet songs. But as my people faded, so did our gods and now they are quite gone."

Caradoc was shocked by this unexpected cynicism but he had no time to respond. Bowerman's tone altered completely.

"Well... enough of that. The sun is up and you must accomplish your task and be back here by dusk. Are you ready?"

They were. Bowerman briefly recounted Findhorn's instructions but there was no need. When a subject attracted Caradoc's interest his memory of it was faultless and every last detail of Findhorn's plan was imprinted indelibly upon his mind. He fingered the phial of liquid in his inside pocket. Bowerman had forced the entrance door while the others slept. There was nothing to delay them further.

Bowerman embraced them all for a moment and then they were gone, into the cool dank tunnel, wide and dimly lit at first but soon narrower and almost completely dark. Along the walls bulged enormous mosses and other nameless subterranean plants which hung from the roof of the tunnel like trails of slime crisscrossing the surfaces, as if to mark their path like an army of giant snails over curtains of seaweed. Five minutes or so into the tunnel and the natural light had faded almost completely. Caradoc now triumphantly produced the nugget of osmundacea. Its light seemed fainter away from its mist-wrapped home but it would do. In the anaemic glow of the moss the pendulous vegetation took on a ghostly hue and Caradoc felt again the sense of unease he had experienced at the rising of the sun. He had walked into the open land of the deadliest creature in his little world; the hand need only close to crush him. He suddenly longed for the company of his father – he had always seemed to Caradoc invincible in battle, a match for any Simian – and his mother, who sat in safety at Grimspound miles to the southeast. But she might not be safe for long if he could not accomplish the dangerous task set for him; and so he must go on without them.

Now the tunnel became so narrow that Hamilcar was called upon to display his excavatory skills. Their path was blocked by numerous little hillocks of earth and rubble. Their presence warned of another, as yet unforeseen, danger, for the tunnel had plainly collapsed in places and might do so again. Hamilcar must proceed carefully for fear of provoking another slip. But the problem of collapsing sets was one with which every self-respecting brock builder was familiar and Hamilcar was a master of the craft. Their progress was slowed but within an hour or so the debris had begun to disperse and their course became clear.

But now other dangers presented themselves. The tunnel ahead was clean, pristine in fact, and utterly denuded of any form of life, whether plant or animal. It had been efficiently and systematically cleansed. And what was more it was lit, brightly illuminated by great firebrands placed at intervals along the walls; none was extinguished which suggested regular tending. They had passed from the disused outer reaches of the Wizard Lord's fortress into the active centre of his operations. Here were Simians and, worse, the tunnels reeked of them. The risk of detection was enhanced by the proliferation of smaller tunnels branching off in all directions. Some were at ground level; others joined their own tunnel at differing levels in the rocky wall, their black openings appearing to hang in the rock face like gaping mouths. Any number of Simians might have lurked therein utterly unseen. On one occasion they heard the sound of harsh, rasping Simian voices percolating through the tunnel network. They stood motionless, unable to locate the source of the sound. Was their passage blocked by a Simian patrol or were they being followed? It was impossible to tell. But the voices sounded only once and then faded away into silence. The group stood motionless for some minutes, straining their ears for the slightest sound. But except for the constant drip-dripping of slimy subterranean waters, there was nothing. They continued cautiously onwards.

An added hazard now faced them: the risk of straying from the appointed path. On several occasions the main tunnel split into several branches of roughly equivalent size. Here the company stopped and poured for some minutes over the old map. A number of lesser forks lay before the final fork, that which Findhorn believed led by one route to the teeming dungeons of their enemy in which many of their captive friends languished, and by the other to the lonely and forgotten prison of the strange and sinister object of their quest. If Findhorn's information was correct, the former would be crawling with Simian guards. To take that way would mean inevitable capture. But the latter course was unguarded. The mind of the Lord of the Northmoor had ceased to dwell upon his predecessor and he no longer visited his living tomb even to gloat. Findhorn's intelligence was correct, and three and a half hours after they had first stepped out of the sunlight the three intruders stood at the crucial crossroads. The map, utterly reliable so far, was now deficient, as its makers, though warlike, had less need for dungeons than did their enemy. But Findhorn had learnt that the road they must avoid fell at first and then rose into the lower reaches of the castle. The road to Magog rose at first and then fell away to the mountain's very roots. And this was the route they took – two children and a badger – down a steep, cold, perilous tunnel into the presence of the most dangerous creature any of them had ever faced.

*

As Caradoc and his companions had entered the tunnel under the mountain that morning a small band of their fellows slipped unnoticed from their cave and began a furtive descent into the poisoned vale below. Findhorn had watched the lights of the Simian horde sent to confront them pass beneath their hill and away to the south. There was much he needed to know. How soon would they return if they did not encounter any immediate opposition? Would they march on to attack the Moorlander villages of the South? How numerous were the slaves toiling in the valley? How many Simians guarded them and how easily could they be freed? If free, were they in a fit state to render any assistance?

Findhorn resolved to take with him Polycanthus, Lemuella, Arken and Brand. Polycanthus was no doubt chosen for his fleetness of foot – the quicker to bring news back to the cave if they were detected. The two fathers, frantic with worry for the welfare of their children, had begun to irritate the less patient members of their company with their constant fretting. The foray would take their mind off their fears. And Lemuella could take out any unsuspecting enemies they might stumble across before they even knew she was there.

They took a steep narrow path to the east of the mountain. Its gradient quickly brought them within sight of the suffering workers and their worst fears were confirmed. Most of the slaves were indeed Moorlanders, although there were also men of darker hue from distant climes – slaves captured and brought from afar. Many toiled above the ground, carrying or dragging great loads of unmentionable substances for transportation to the Wizard Lord's manufactory beneath the mountain. Some staggered and fainted beneath the weight and the searing heat rising from the furnaces in the mines below. Those who did so were brought to their feet with the blistering hogweed whips. But these were the lucky ones. For in the subterranean mines of the underworld only the strongest slaves survived for long. Those who fell were thrown into the furnaces and their ranks replenished from the dungeons. They now understood their enemies' constant need for captives.

The little band surveyed the sickening spectacle from behind some suitably dense gorse. As Findhorn counted the Simian guards, Polycanthus scrutinised the anguished faces of the captives and gazed straight into the face of his old friend Didymus. He was astounded. He had last seen Didymus at Drizzlecombe on the evening before they left. Polycanthus whimpered in panic.

"Findhorn, by the Goddess, Findhorn… what have they done to Drizzlecombe?"

"Is he a Drizzlecomber? Which one?"

Findhorn endeavoured to hide his concern, but he too was plainly worried.

"That one… down there… Didymus. He was there the night before we left. By the Goddess, is there anyone left?"

"Alright, calm down… I'm sure there's some other explanation," Findhorn reassured.

"Look, we've got to try and speak to him. You're the quickest and nimblest, Polycanthus. Do you feel up to it?"

"Certainly," Polycanthus replied.

"Good. Now there's only one guard for your friend and five others, and he's down there by that cart." Findhorn

189

pointed to a strange covered wagon into which two other Moorlanders were loading bulging sacks, seemingly larger than themselves.

"Slip down on the far side and call to him from behind that rock. Ask him how he got to be here and how many prisoners there are locked up in the castle. But don't take any risks. If you can't get close enough to him or the guard shows an interest then come straight back again – as quickly and quietly as possible."

"Don't worry, I'll be Polycanthus o' the Wisp," he laughed nervously. "And, Lemuella, be ready to put an arrow in any guard who shows an interest."

"With pleasure," she replied and loosened an arrow.

Polycanthus drifted off into the heather to the right of the path and disappeared from view for some minutes. He soon reappeared behind the appointed "rock". His body leant forward, straining in the direction of his forlorn friend. He hissed his friend's name softly but intently: "Didymus, Didymus. Here!"

Didymus glanced around in the direction of the rock. His face was a confused blend of terror and desperation. His attention rested on the rock for a second only and returned immediately to the task in hand. The horror of detection was evident in his cowed demeanour. Polycanthus hissed his name again. But he did not react. He hissed louder but still without response. But the next sound uttered by Polycanthus alerted every creature for hundreds of yards around. A shrill scream of mingled pain and fear met the air and Polycanthus' contorted body toppled from behind the rock, a Simian arrow embedded deep in his ankle. Simultaneously two baying Simians sprang to greet it. There was plainly no intention of taking any prisoners and Lemuella felled the first Simian, and Brand and Arken sprang forward to intercept the second, followed less nimbly by Findhorn.

The remaining guard, no doubt baffled by the sudden appearance of these two burly and uncharacteristically pugilistic Moorlanders, hesitated and was promptly cut down where it stood. In seconds a Simian stood on every rock. They were utterly surrounded, with no hope of escape.

CHAPTER EIGHTEEN

THE SORCERER AWAKES

The descent to the dungeons was steep. In places it was stepped but where it was not, the going was painfully slow. Caradoc and his friends proceeded in single file and hand in hand. The darkness was so profound that even the osmundacea made little impression on it.

But the way was not long. They had travelled no more than a few hundred yards when their path began to brighten, illuminated by strands of light from a pinpoint source at the end of the tunnel. As they drew nearer to the source, the radiance appeared wan and strangely familiar, and the tunnel began to widen. It opened out into a great chamber, akin to, but immeasurably greater in size than, that in which Caradoc had first marvelled at the beauty of the glowing moss and been seduced by the wiles of its keeper. The three tiny travellers stepped out into its perilous vastness from the dark, cool safety of the tunnel with only the vaguest notion of what might lie therein.

So huge was it in fact that those entering from the eastern tunnel could not glimpse its western end. Caradoc's awed intake of breath bounced audibly from megalithic wall to megalithic wall. Ellie could not resist commenting.

"His little heart… how it beats," she chided. "It'll wake the sorcerer on its own."

Caradoc refused to be goaded. "What's that smell?" he enquired, changing the subject. "It smells like the witch."

"It isn't the witch, it's the fungus," replied Ellie. "It's growing over there." She pointed to a hollow in the rock face on the northern wall. The pure white fungus could clearly be seen growing in clumps. Caradoc approached it, enthralled.

"Do you realise that a portion of that as small as the half moon on the nail of your little finger could kill you?"

"Only if you eat it," retorted Ellie unimpressed.

Undaunted by her flippancy he bent over the nearest cluster to scrutinise it. The fungus was so white it appeared almost blue. He was tempted to touch it but knew he would be washing his hands for days if he did.

"So, this must be where he got it from," he thought to himself aloud. There was no reply. He turned and looked behind him. Ellie and Hamilcar stood side by side, staring transfixed at the rock wall of the hollow a little above his head. He followed the gaze. For seconds the three of them gawped, speechless.

Ellie broke the silence. "Do you mean him?" she asked hesitantly.

"No," said Caradoc quietly, "his star pupil."

At first sight the wall appeared to be enveloped beneath some other species of fungus – large amorphous and woody. It shared the brooding horror of the white angel fungus but lacked its deadly charm. A second glance betrayed its true nature – human, or something very like it; certainly not fungal. The arms and legs were spreadeagled and they and the trunk were held immobile by thick strands of knotted timber, like the roots of ivy but far thicker, which appeared to grow from the rock face. Between the twisted branches they could glimpse the wizened, wrinkled skin of the creature held within. Its hue varied from a dull yellow to the deepest ochre as if far advanced in decay and its leather-like texture was softened by a smattering of fine black hair. There protruded above the woody bonds the creature's head, an oval mass separated from the shoulders by no discernible neck. The skin of the head was similarly leathery and from deep within it peered two empty eyes – open but lifeless. Lifeless too were the dry formless flaps that formed the lips of the creature's twisted mouth.

Ellie was the first to overcome her sense of nausea.

"He looks like he's been dead for years. We'll never wake him. And he's so small. He's no bigger than you. What use can he be to us?"

Caradoc was inclined to agree with her. But he felt he

must maintain his support for Findhorn, in public at least, despite his waning confidence.

"We'll wake him," he said as firmly as he was able. "Findhorn would not have sent us on such a dangerous errand for nothing, but how do we get up there?"

"Well, if we must try… Hamilcar, make a back. Caradoc, climb on top of him," Ellie snapped and Hamilcar made no move to comply.

"Go on, old friend, you might as well do as she says," said Caradoc, accompanied by appropriately demonstrative gesticulations.

"He knows what you mean. Make him get on with it," said Ellie.

"Well, he isn't a slave. You should speak to him with more respect."

Before she could answer they were both distracted by a low growling behind them. The badger had already made a back and was impatient for them to get on with it. Caradoc stepped onto his broad shoulders and tottered there precariously. As nimbly as a treecreeper Ellie clambered up his back and perched astride his shoulders.

She glanced to her left and stared straight into the face of the Sorcerer.

"The antidote – the phial – give it to me."

Caradoc carefully passed the precious liquid into her hands. There was silence for a moment.

"What do I do with it?" she said.

"Oh by the Goddess… you should have listened to Findhorn."

"But I didn't… and I'm sure you did. So tell me."

"You pour half in his mouth and the other half in his ears."

"I can't see his ears. Perhaps he hasn't any. I bet Findhorn never thought of that."

"Don't be stupid. Of course he has." He carefully passed the lump of osmundacea to her.

"It's not enough. Pass me some more."

"What on earth are you talking about?" exclaimed Caradoc in exasperation. "More – I haven't got any more."

"Of course you have," she retorted with maddening levity. "I'll get some myself." She skipped back to the ground as rapidly as she had ascended and disappeared into the semi-darkness. Within seconds she was back, a large clump of the glowing moss in each hand. It was paler than Caradoc's own and whiter – but undoubtedly osmundacea.

Caradoc now understood the familiarity of the light at the end of the tunnel. The similarity between the Wizard Lord's mountain and Vixana's tor was uncanny. He would not have been in the least surprised to meet her here.

The living pyramid was reassembled and Ellie climbed again towards the sinister sleeping head. Fully illuminated, the workings of decay were vivid and horrible to behold. Ellie realised she would have to perform her task quickly before she lost the will to perform it at all. Bracing herself, she grabbed the lower lip between her fingers, fully expecting it to turn to dust in her hands. But it was tough and rubbery and seemed never to have had life in it. She emptied a substantial portion of the phial's contents into its mouth and then held the lips firmly together for a moment. A little seeped from each corner but most found its way in the direction intended. The rest she shared equally between each ear.

Initially, there was no reaction. But as she slithered to the ground over the tired shoulders of her companions, the creature stirred behind her. They all three scuttled away a few yards and then turned. Still backing away, they half expected to confront the twisted form of the Sorcerer loping after them in hot pursuit, shedding his shattered bonds as he came.

"Surely it won't work that quickly," exclaimed Caradoc. "Findhorn reckoned it would take ages."

And Findhorn was right; the creature had not woken. But perhaps the antidote was beginning to do its job and the Sorcerer's long sleep would soon end, for his body twitched and shuddered convulsively for some seconds before lapsing again into immobility.

"Come on, let's get out of here," said Ellie quietly. The others needed no encouragement. They quickly regained the mouth of the tunnel and began the steep ascent back towards the sunlight. The thought of Bowerman's strong protective arm waiting at the tunnel's end sped their steps and they made much quicker progress back up the steep, winding path than they had made down it.

All about them was full of noises: the slow oozing and dripping of subterranean waters, the rumbling of distant rock falls and the echo of their own tramping feet and pounding breath. There were other noises too, distant and indistinct at first but soon unmistakeable and drawing closer: the cackle of Simian chatter advancing down the path to meet them. The realisation that their escape route was blocked and impassable instilled in them something approaching despair. The sudden loss of hope was more difficult to bear than the sense of immediate danger. They sat upon the floor, head in hands, while the distant voices drew nearer. Even Ellie would have welcomed the guidance of Findhorn now.

After a moment Caradoc said, "Did you see any side tunnels on the way up?"

"No," replied Ellie.

"Nor did I. We will have to go back through the chamber."

"But what about the Sorcerer. What if he is awake? And what about your map? Are there no tunnels on that?"

Caradoc did not need to look. He knew there were none. "We have to take the risk," he said. "And why should the Sorcerer mean us any harm? We have helped him."

"You didn't see his face," said Ellie. "I can't imagine him returning any favours."

She had to agree, however, that there was no choice. So they turned and picked their way down the narrow tunnel, with even greater reluctance than before. Findhorn's map disclosed at least three tunnels serving the great chamber: their own and two others at the chamber's western end. But the map was far from clear as to which they should take. Above and beyond the great chamber lay the halls of the Wizard Lord. There they must not go. Their best hope was to seek out other uncharted passageways, which must surely exist amidst the myriad of tunnels, and thereby find their way below the realm of their enemy and away to freedom.

They reached the chamber only too quickly and huddled nervously at the entrance for some moments. Ellie was in favour of creeping along the far wall, feeling their way in the darkness. Caradoc disagreed; without light they would spend as long in the chamber as the Sorcerer. The only thing for it was to slip through the chamber as quickly and inconspicuously as possible and hope the creature still slept.

Hamilcar went first, his jaws bared and his claws poised to sell his life dearly should the need arise. Caradoc and Ellie followed, a little less pugnaciously, behind. As they drew near the centre of the chamber each scrutinised the eastern wall, hoping to pick out the dim form of the Sorcerer still safely entwined in his woody straightjacket. Ellie, keenest-eyed of the three, was the first to pick out the shattered twines dangling redundantly from the chamber wall.

"He's gone," she said in as calm a voice as she could muster. All three froze. They stood motionless for a moment in complete silence, broken only by a barely perceptible growl from Hamilcar, which Caradoc felt rather than heard. Somewhere in the pitch blackness beyond the little circle of light thrown out nervously by the moss, the Sorcerer surely watched them.

"What shall we do?" whispered Caradoc eventually. The sound seemed to echo like thunder around the chamber.

"We might as well run for it," replied Ellie with an air of resignation.

Caradoc thought for a moment. "No, we must continue as we are. If he's still in the chamber then he'll see us – but that's better than running straight into him. It's not far to the other side."

Ellie could see the sense in this, even though she slightly objected to his authoritarian tone. He was beginning, unconsciously perhaps, to assume the role of leader; and she was beginning rather more consciously to resent it. But at least he was not the dim-witted ditherer she had first taken him for. So she swallowed her pride and took the proffered hand and followed boy and badger into the darkness.

As the vast mass of the chamber's western wall loomed up before them, Caradoc was reminded of the passage through the wood in the valley of the fifth river. Within the impenetrable blackness beyond the wood's edge had lurked the bear. He could see them but, immense though he was, they could not see him, so it might be with the Sorcerer. He could choose his time and his victim at his leisure.

But if the Sorcerer was watching them from the darkness then this was plainly not his time. They reached the western wall without incident and were now faced with the crucial choice of exit tunnel. The tunnel mouths, though small, were easily identifiable. Although dark, their blackness was a little less profound than the surrounding rock; lights burned in the distant reaches of both. Caradoc peered into the nearest opening. Two motionless forms lay huddled together a short distance inside. He surveyed them silently for a moment for any sign of life. Then gesturing to Hamilcar to back him up, he tiptoed softly forward for a closer look.

As he had suspected, the forms were the bodies of Simians. They were quite dead but there was not the slightest evidence of a struggle. The possibility of their both dying simultaneously of natural causes strained the credulity of even a naive young Moorlander. He crouched to examine the corpses in the glow of the moss.

"By the Goddess," exclaimed Ellie from behind him. "What are they?"

On the forehead of each Simian was a mark – an indentation almost. The skull appeared depressed, forced back into the creature's head to a distance of a half-inch or more. The core of the compression was black but there was no burning or other sign of violence.

"It's the thumbprint of the Sorcerer," replied Caradoc darkly.

He attempted a reassuring smile but secretly he was appalled by the power that could depress a Simian skull with such cool, clinical efficiency. But at least the discovery solved one problem: it told them which way to go. The Sorcerer would know the tunnel network intimately and surely after an aeon of impotency would take the route which would bring him most quickly to the object of his hatred. They must go the other way.

CHAPTER NINETEEN

THE THRONE
ROOM

The chosen path fell away at first but after an hour or so it began to rise and continued to do so steadily until the travellers began to fear they had taken the wrong route. There were no connecting tunnels and so there was no option but to continue. An hour more and the tunnel opened out into a wide, flat-bottomed corridor illuminated by great firebrands suspended at intervals along the walls. The floor was strewn with debris of broken masonry and ancient decaying weaponry and armour; and upon the disorder there gazed down the huge granite likenesses of the kings of the old halls. A broken nose here or a missing ear there did not distract from the majesty of the immense figures.

There were upwards of thirty in all, each perched on a flat granite pedestal. Each pedestal bore upon it the faded outline of a bounding figure: the hare god of the men of the Northmoor – the "old runner" in the common tongue.

As Ellie stamped her feet impatiently, Caradoc and Hamilcar stood in awe before the silent kings. Hares had haunted the moor for 100,000 years, it was said – longer even than badgers and a long age before the coming of the Easterners. But their forms had been empty for a generation, their owners slaughtered mercilessly by the men from the East for no reason other than fear – fear and mistrust of a creature which could teem over the rolling hills entirely unseen. They killed with poison a creature which they could not see to slay by hand. The badgers had loved the hares and despite their aloof elusiveness the badgers believed the hares loved them. The striped snout of this badger ran with tears, and such was the poignancy of the moment that Ellie gulped back the devastating sarcasm she had been preparing and looked on respectfully.

At the end of the chamber a narrow flight of broken steps ascended into the shadows above the light cast by the firebrands. It was the only way out and as they negotiated its precarious angles they prayed it might lead to some unguarded exit high on the tor's remote western face.

But they were soon back on level ground as the steep stairway gave way to yet another untended tunnel. Here there were no firebrands but sufficient light seeped into the tunnel from somewhere to render the use of the moss unnecessary. As they made progress a low, distant hum, vague and muffled, at first evolved gradually into the faint but distant sound of human voices.

"We must go back," said Ellie immediately. "We're walking straight into his grasp."

Caradoc predictably disagreed. "No, I don't agree, if we go back, we could end up wandering inside the mountain forever. Those voices could be coming from anywhere."

Ellie did not look convinced. The voices sounded close but she knew how effectively sound percolated through the rock fissures.

"Alright, we'll go on. But don't blame me if we're soon guests of His Malevolence the Sorcerer. He won't be as easy to say goodnight to as dear old Vixana."

Caradoc shivered at the memory. And yet although he knew full well that the creature through those halls they wandered was altogether more potent and more deadly than the Witch of Vixen Tor, he could not bring himself to fear what he did not know. It reassured him to know that there at least he had the advantage of Ellie. She feared the unknown while he did not. But should they confront the Lord of the Northmoor? Who would feel the greater terror then? he wondered. He hoped his constancy would not be put to the test.

With every step they took the voices grew until they appeared to envelop the walls on every side. Light poured into the tunnel from a large fissure in the floor ahead of them, and Hamilcar, taking the lead as always, halted at its edge and peered in. Immediately his broad back spread itself against the floor, his neck hairs bristled and his low growl told his companions there was trouble ahead.

Caradoc and Ellie drew alongside him and gazed down at the astounding spectacle beneath their feet. The throne room into which they looked was crowded with figures. The walls were lined with Simians of all shapes and sizes, from short, squat, bow-legged barrels to great broad-shouldered beasts like miniature Bowermans. Amongst them lurked a smattering of disreputable-looking men, all armed to the teeth and most grinning hideously about them. At the far northern end of the hall reclined the great leader, leering smugly down at his vassals.

Caradoc scrutinised the seated figure closely. Even at this distance it had about it an undoubted air of familiarity. This was not his first encounter with the Lord of the Northmoor. He had narrowly eluded his attentions in Wistman's Wood. He felt again the sensation almost approaching physical pain experienced by all those who looked too long into the Wizard Lord's eyes. On either side of their master crouched two immense square-headed beasts; at least one of them had accompanied its master on his recent foray down the valley of the sixth river.

The thought crossed Caradoc's mind that he could have saved his companions a great deal of trouble, and also a few lives as well, had he reacted more resolutely on the night in the twisted wood. A well-placed Moorlander arrow might have done the trick. But another glance at the face of his adversary told him that this was not a foe likely to succumb to his puny endeavours. He need not feel that he had let his friends down. The Lord of the Northmoor was more than a match for him.

He strained to follow the glance of the Wizard Lord, pressing his breast against the rock and craning his neck forward to peer backwards into the main body of the hall. His gaze fell upon the familiar dome of Findhorn. Beside the old wizard stood his father, Lemuella and Polycanthus, and behind them loomed the unmistakable bulk of Brand. The little group was encircled by a phalanx of spear-wielding Simians and Caradoc's first impulse was to drop to the floor alongside his friends to help fend off the imminent attack. But no attack came and although Caradoc could not hear what he was saying, Findhorn was plainly deep in disputation with the enemy. The Wizard Lord threw back his hooded head and laughed sardonically – and his minions followed suit in lemming-like fashion.

His inclination was still to go to his father's side. His task was complete, the Sorcerer was awake, although where he was now the Goddess only knew but if they were in no immediate danger then perhaps it was best to sit and wait and bide his time. The decision, however, was taken out of his hands.

A frantic torrent of scratching erupted beside him and from the corner of his eye Caradoc glimpsed the striped snout of the badger plummeting downwards into the void below, closely followed by the rest of his body. Hamilcar landed in a crumpled heap on the floor below. The assembled Simians, so nonchalant when confronting a surrounded and stationary enemy, faltered in the face of this strange airborne assailant. But their panic was momentary and as the breathless badger dragged himself up off the floor, a few of the bolder and more reckless advanced ominously towards him.

Hamilcar was in danger and Caradoc must join him. As he dropped to the floor Ellie fell with him. Caradoc flourished his Moorlander blade and waved it intimidatingly at the foremost Simian. A number of the fainter-hearted amongst the advancing enemy again baulked before the unusual manner of their arrival – but not their leader, a giant, long-limbed, squinting fellow who bore down on Caradoc unabashed.

Bravely, if somewhat foolishly, Caradoc stepped forward to meet him. The Simian flourished his curved blade, at a height that Caradoc could not reach to parry. His only hope was to strike from below. The creature was almost upon him when it staggered sideways and crumpled in an untidy heap at the feet of the now revitalised Hamilcar who immediately sprang upon him. There was no need, however, for Arken's blow had done the job.

Seeing their children in danger, Brand and Arken had brushed aside the thin line of surrounding Simians and borne down upon the gaunt, long-limbed fellow like a buzzard on a young rabbit.

It seemed to Caradoc that every Simian in the hall then descended upon them. He now discovered the source of the reputations enjoyed by his father and Brand in the ranks of the Moorlander military. The Simian assault was repulsed time and time again. Brand and Arken formed the centre of the defence with the powerful Hamilcar to their right and the agile and skilful Polycanthus to their left. Caradoc and Ellie occasionally nipped between them to deal out a series of ungentlemanly lunges at unsuspecting foes.

Caradoc also took upon himself the responsibility for protecting Findhorn. He was sure that there must be any number of cowardly Simians who would much prefer to concentrate their assault upon the frail old man than the far more hazardous business of a confrontation with the front line. But strangely, none did. Findhorn did not seem to make any real contribution to the defence other than possibly by hovering about on the longer, more exposed, flank of the Moorlander group which thereby remained inexplicably trouble free. The Simians seemed to concentrate their attack on Lemuella whose lightning flow of arrows was taking a toll on the Simian ranks but, protected by Arken and Brand, they could not get near her. But her stock of arrows was swiftly running out. Caradoc could not guess what hidden power the Mage possessed – nothing about Findhorn surprised him anymore – but what did surprise him was how the Simians seemed universally aware of it; perhaps they were not as stupid as they looked.

A smattering of Simian bodies now littered the ground between the gallant defenders and the hordes of their assailants. However, not one of Caradoc and his fellows had any doubts as to the final outcome. Seven could not defeat 700. Hamilcar had already suffered a stab wound to the shoulder and Polycanthus was limping from a mace blow to the leg. It was then, as the next onslaught was about to commence, that a series of events occurred, more astounding even than the sight of Findhorn's bald head from the tunnel above.

In the gloom of the hall's far side, two immense ancient doors were set in the wall. All of a sudden these great wooden portals were thrust apart. Through them lurked the outline of a bloodied Simian guard. Above and to either side of the creature's form there loomed the outline of a much vaster being. As the Simian moved into the light his true terror became apparent. He attempted to cry out some message to his friends congregated in the chamber but the sound was strangled in his throat as he was poleaxed spectacularly by the giant behind him.

At first, the little band of defenders greeted this new turn of events with dismay. The huge shape in the doorway could only be some hitherto unknown servant of the Wizard Lord. What little hope remained to them began to evaporate in the heart of each. But as the creature followed its victims into the light, Caradoc's sinking spirits stirred within him and erupted with an involuntary whoop of joy. Even the usually sullen Brand indulged himself in a little squeal of excitement. For the giant standing before them, blinking in the glare of the burning firebrands, was their good friend Bowerman. The snug, green, distant valleys of home, which had seemed so remote only a few moments ago, now seemed a little closer.

Bowerman seemed an intimidating figure indeed as he glowered about him at the ranks of the wilting enemy. The Simian panic was frenzied to the point of self-injury in their efforts to place their fellows between themselves and the newcomer. Caradoc scrutinised the Giganticus closely, wondering whether he intended to attack the Simians or merely scowl at them. He looked again into those strange, sad, sunken eyes and marvelled that their owner could inspire fear in anyone. But inspire fear in the Simians he undoubtedly did.

Moreover, he had not come alone. From the shadows behind him three more figures loomed up. The first of these was unmistakable; Caradoc would recognise the ungainly long-snouted profile of Wolfsbane anywhere. Alongside the badger strode Fortinbras and with him his father's good friend Hama.

For a moment the warring parties confronted one another uneasily, each waiting for the other to make the first move. Then a din arose at the north end of the hall and the crowded Simian cohorts surged forward again. This was not a renewed assault, however; the startled monkeys were scattering in the path of someone they feared even more than Bowerman. Their ranks opened and the Lord of the Northmoor strode out into the no-man's land. Beside the Giganticus he seemed a very puny figure and Caradoc felt for a moment that Bowerman might end all their troubles with a single blow. But Bowerman himself had no such misconceptions. He looked into the eyes of his enemy and stepped back.

The Wizard Lord beamed about him; it was good that his own people should see that his enemies' most formidable warrior feared him as much as they did.

He laughed a thin, sweet, evil laugh. "Now for some

fun," he sneered. "Let's see what this big oaf is made of. Let's send him the way of all his fellows."

He raised an arm behind him and, without turning, snapped his fingers in the direction of the dais. Every eye, save his, looked towards it. In the semi-darkness behind the Wizard Lord's throne a creature stirred. Caradoc had never set eyes on the giant Simian before but the tales of his slaughter of the Grimspounders had reached the ears of every Moorlander. Under long shadows thrown by the firebrands he seemed vaster even than he was.

The Simian loped down the corridor formed by his master and approached Bowerman. Somewhat surprisingly he seemed a little less tall than the Giganticus, his immense torso dragged downwards by his round-shouldered, stooping gait. His arms sprouting from his shoulders like great tree trunks would have scraped the ground had they been remotely straight; but in texture and form they recalled to Caradoc the twisted trees of Wistman's Wood. The Simian was unarmed and as their host plainly had single combat in mind it appeared that a wrestling match was imminent.

The Lord of the Northmoor snapped his fingers again. Arms bearers now appeared – two pairs of burly Simians each struggling under the weight of an enormous broadsword. So colossal were they that they could only have been forged for the likes of the two adversaries, for no ordinary mortal could wield them. One was conveyed with difficulty into the hands of the Simian; the other was offered to Bowerman.

"Now, let's all be civilised about this, shall we?" oozed

the Wizard Lord with obvious relish. "We don't want to make a nasty mess. These two can sort it out. My best Simian against the last Giganticus. And we can all sit back and enjoy the spectacle."

"I am not the last Giganticus," said Bowerman softly but firmly.

"But of course you are, old chap. Where would they hide another one like you?"

Bowerman faltered visibly and his head bowed. Findhorn now thought the time ripe for his own contribution. If Bowerman was to fight the giant Simian it was important that his mind should be on matters pugilistic and not the survival of his race.

The Mage drew alongside Caradoc. "Did you do it? Did it work?" he whispered.

Amidst the turmoil Caradoc had forgotten for a moment the purpose of his quest.

"What... what did I do?"

"The phial," hissed Findhorn impatiently. "Did you use it?"

The memory of Magog came flooding back. "Yes," he cried with a mixture of pride and excitement, "and it worked... he's awake."

"Then where is he?"

"I've no idea... he just vanished."

Findhorn patted his young friend reassuringly on the back. "Well done," he whispered. "I knew I had made the right choice."

Caradoc watched the old mage as he strode confidently through the ranks of the enemy. They fell away before his face as they had before their own master. He drew alongside Bowerman.

"You don't need to do it," he said loudly and demonstratively. "There's enough of us to battle our way out together," and then, and more intimately, "You know the tales as well as I do – the tales of Gigantici on the moors beyond the southern seas. Caradoc and his friends have done their job. Let's go and find them."

But their host was not to be put off so easily. He wanted blood.

"Ah, I wondered what your role was, old man," he interjected. "Why such a crack fighting force had seen fit to bring a scarecrow with them." He paused a moment to milk the laughter of his slaves. "You must be the brains of the outfit… I suppose someone had to be…" – more dutiful sniggering – "Well, if you are the brains, you'll reassure this musclebound dunderhead that only the slaying of my Simian will see his friends leave my realm alive. So he'd better accept my kind offer."

The Wizard Lord paused and for a moment there was silence as the two scrutinised one another curiously. It occurred to Caradoc how alike they were. Their ages were quite different, of course, and one was good and the other evil; but there must be many mysteries that they alone of all the dwellers on the moor understood.

"I accept it," said Bowerman quietly. He took the proffered weapon from the patient bearers, who backed off, relieved to be rid of its great weight. The ease with which he bore it amazed friend and foe alike. He raised it above his head and advanced. The Simian flourished his own blade above his head with equal facility and the two blades came crashing together like the roar of a mountain torrent. Both protagonists staggered backwards under the force of the blow. Ominously it seemed to Caradoc that of the two, Bowerman staggered the further. Four more great strokes followed and their echoes rang throughout the hall. The Simian was the stronger but Bowerman had the greater skill, and slowly and with each lunge the balance of the Simian grew ever more precarious. Finally he missed his swing and pitched forward. Bowerman's scything blade entered his side and the Simian's legs gave way beneath him. As he fell, his wildly flailing blade nicked the knee of his victorious opponent. But it was the last blow he would ever strike.

CHAPTER TWENTY

HOW THE
SORCERER HAD
HIS REVENGE

If the Lord of the Northmoor felt anything approaching shock or regret as his lesser slaves carried away the body of his fallen champion he did not show it. He even managed to summon up a characteristic sarcasm for their ineffectual efforts. But a little interest was kindled in this ragtag of intruders. Why had they come? What did they hope to achieve? And who was the grizzled old man who looked oddly familiar and in whom his companions seemed to place so much trust? He must investigate further. He would ooze some more.

"There you are, your freedom assured," he beamed

without the least intention that it should be. "And your champion unscathed and fit to fight another day."

He turned his attention to Findhorn who was tending to the knee of the not entirely unscathed Bowerman. "My friend," he announced jocularly, "we are two of a kind. Let us talk in my private rooms and enjoy a moorland draught or two." He attempted a knowing wink but produced something approaching a sinister leer.

Findhorn felt only revulsion for this contrived amiability. Yet perhaps he might learn something. At least it would delay the inevitable final confrontation – hopefully for long enough to enable the liberated one to do his work. He had not the slightest hope that the Lord of the Northmoor would keep his word.

"Yes, that would be nice," he replied with irony worthy of his host.

"Wonderful… delightful… This way."

As Findhorn turned to follow he looked back in the direction of Caradoc. At first Caradoc thought he was waving goodbye but it very soon occurred to him that he was being invited to tag along. He glanced at his father, who nodded his consent. Arken mistrusted the intentions of the Lord of the Northmoor as much as the next Moorlander. But he also knew that although he would have died to save his son from harm, he was undoubtedly safer with Findhorn than with his father. However, as Caradoc trotted after the Mage, Arken had second thoughts and decided the safest thing to do was to gatecrash.

All three followed their treacherous host to the north end of the chamber, past the dais and through a heavy velvet curtain to a tunnel beyond. It was immediately apparent that they had entered the private quarters of the Lord of the Northmoor. All was opulence. The walls were adorned with gorgeous draperies – the exquisite produce of a distant land – and instead of the hard granite floor of the great chamber, they walked upon fabrics as soft and yielding as a moorland peat bog.

Beyond a second velvet curtain lay the lordly sleeping quarters. It was plain that their enemies' desecration of the moor was yielding him rich dividends, for this, his innermost sanctum, surpassed in luxury Caradoc's wildest imaginings, let alone his experience. Even the men who adorned their pottery with long-nosed fish could not have lived like this. Everything from the green marble floor inlaid with gold and jet to the livery of the Simian attendants was delicious to the eye. But why, Caradoc wondered, did he destroy the natural wonders of the moor to create this private but artificial paradise inside the mountain? It was beyond Caradoc's understanding.

The Wizard Lord strode across the marble floor and draped himself across an enormous chaise longue – a far cry from his own granite stool, Caradoc thought. He rested upon one elbow and surveyed his guests for their reactions to his success. They must at least be impressed – but what he really wanted was envy. He only saw wonder in the eyes of the child.

Caradoc's enthralled gaze strayed beyond the chaise longue to where three marble steps led up to an unseen inner chamber. An exquisite hanging, green and shimmering, concealed the interior from sight. The hanging was delicate, and by the medium of some lost breeze from the world beyond the mountains billowed gently to and fro. As Caradoc watched, the two sides of the fabric parted slightly and he saw into the room beyond. Within a moment the view was gone and the curtain had closed but Caradoc knew now the means by which their salvation might be accomplished.

Behind the curtain in the Wizard Lord's bedchamber stood a great oak chair bedecked with emeralds. It had once been the throne of Magog. Caradoc did not know this, of course, but he did know who sat in it now. He had seen very little of the body of the occupant but what he had seen had sufficed. The scaly green skin covering the domed scalp that protruded above the chair's high back and the hand that rested upon its massive clawed arm could belong to no one else; the Sorcerer had found his way back to the heart of his former kingdom. Caradoc's excitement was palpable; surely the Lord of the Northmoor would feel it. Some mighty stroke was imminent.

The Lord of the Northmoor appeared not to feel it, however. He seemed concerned only with his own magnificence. He snapped his fingers imperiously at the nearest attendant and summoned refreshment. The attendant ascended the three steps and passed through the curtain. Caradoc braced himself for the inevitable expression of horror. There was nothing. Caradoc wondered for a moment whether he had been mistaken – but inside he knew he had not been. The Sorcerer must have despatched the burly Simian attendant with such efficiency that his actions were imperceptible, even to those a few feet away. Caradoc recalled the Simian guard at the exit to the underground chamber and shuddered.

Apparently oblivious to the drama unfolding around him, the present incumbent of the throne under Hangingstone Hill commenced his interrogation.

"So tell me, old man," he began almost pleasantly, "why have you come here," and then more ominously, "when there is so little hope of your ever leaving?"

Findhorn, who could bandy ironies with the best, rose to the occasion.

"We in the Southmoor have heard much of the kindliness and… uh… efficiency of your rule. We came to learn so that we may govern our people better."

"And how right you are to do so. I have heard of your silly meetings, your pointless deliberations – they get you nowhere. You have need of a strong man, to take your decisions for you, to get things done. I have to tell you that your journey northwards was a mistake… one might say a fatal mistake. It was wholly unnecessary, as I had it in mind to pay a visit to you myself – and sort out your little political problems."

This diatribe on the part of their host was interrupted by the return of the Simian attendant – a return which, in Caradoc's mind at least, was wholly unexpected. He stared at the Simian in amazement. Superficially there appeared to be no dramatic transformation, no evidence of frenzied attack, no terminal depressions of the skull. The attendant bore a silver tray and four goblets, just as one would have expected him to do, and he waited dutifully before the reclining person of his master until his services were required.

There was something in his manner, though, that was no longer servile. The stooping, cringing stance of the Simian household attendant was entirely vanished. Instead, the creature stood erect and tall, his eyes staring intently before him. The Wizard Lord was too engrossed in his own opinions to notice.

"Now, tell me, old man," he continued, "why is it that you look so familiar to me… when I am certain we have never met before?"

Caradoc saw his chance to make his own contribution to the sparring. "Because he is the most famous person on the moor. You must have heard the tales your slaves tell of him?" He hoped this would suitably infuriate their host, whom Caradoc was certain would consider himself the most famous person on the moor, for not the least of his vices was vanity. Arken, not wishing to infuriate him at all whilst they were so firmly in his clutches, placed a restraining hand on his son's shoulder.

But it appeared he had no cause for concern, for their host's pleasure in the whole affair did not seem in any way diminished.

"Splendid spirit," he guffawed. "Splendid young fellow… if a little ill-informed. You see before you the principal being, the prime mover of your little world and indeed of many lands beyond it. Each epoch yields its own supreme being, one whose lot it is to mould the lives of those lesser beings with whom he has the misfortune to co-exist. And for these times I am that being; let's drink to it. My goblet, slave!"

He would regret that he did not take the trouble to honour his drinks-bearer with a glance. Had he done so, he would surely have noticed that the metamorphosis was failing. If this was shapechanging it did not last long or perhaps the Sorcerer's command of the art had declined through the long sleep. The grey Simian scalp of the drinks-bearer was resuming the scaly green hue Caradoc had espied through the billowing drapes only minutes before. He could not believe that he alone of the occupiers of the room had noticed.

The Wizard Lord's great golden goblet was thrust into his outstretched hand and he sank a great draught. The others sipped gingerly at the more modest receptacles offered them.

"Now, what I am to do with you?" their host droned on between gulps. "Do you die horribly or do I send you home to convince your friends of the benefits of my rule? Perhaps a little of each, with the former dependent upon the success of the latter."

He threw back his head for another draught but strangely the contents of his glass splashed against his left cheek and shoulder. His characteristic expression of enormous unshakeable self-satisfaction was transformed in an instant to doubt and confusion. He rose unsteadily to his feet and blinked stupidly around him to discover the source of his undoing. His three guests appeared innocent and unchanged. He glanced to his right and looked straight into the face of his ancient enemy. He knew now the scale of his own misjudgement; he had sustained and nourished within his own house the only power with the means to overthrow him and spurned 10,000 opportunities to end it. Now, with exquisite irony, it had returned to use against him those same deadly agents he himself had used against it. Even as the white angel coursed through his veins he could see the poetic justice of it all. He still mused on its poetry as the vigour left his limbs and the spasms reached his abdomen. His face grew hideous with agony and he pitched forward headlong and insensible.

There could now be no doubt as to the identity of the poisoner. The gloating, grinning gargoyle of a face relishing the final works of the fungus was unmistakably that of Magog. As the last agonised convulsion subsided in the fallen body, the Sorcerer stepped forward, scooped it up with the ease of a mother cradling a newborn and made for a hitherto unnoticed doorway in the chamber's northern wall. The remaining Simian attendants made no attempt to stop him. Only Arken made as if to follow and put his hand to the hilt of his sword as if to draw. He approached the Sorcerer from behind and made no sound. The Sorcerer perceived him nevertheless and turned upon him, crouching like a springing cat. The lipless mouth gaped and the creature hissed threateningly, a sound more reptilian than feline that froze the blood of all who heard it. Arken stood his ground. The hiss was followed by a foul expectoration – a dark brown slime that fell short of its intended victim but smoked and sizzled on the marble floor before him. Arken was no coward but neither was he a fool. He backed off just as Findhorn was about to restrain him. The Sorcerer, still cradling the body of his victim, disappeared through the curtained doorway and was gone.

CHAPTER TWENTY-ONE

AFTERWARDS

C haos reigned in the great chamber. By the time
Caradoc and his friends returned to it the story
of their master's demise had been relayed to
every Simian ear by the fleeing attendants. Most of
the older Simians remembered Magog, and despite the
passing of the years their fear of him burned fierce and
undiminished. He would surely have something to say
to those of his followers who had served his treacherous
successor as readily as they had served him.

They panicked. Some cowered in obscure corners;
some fled into the dark tunnels beneath the hill where they
hoped the Sorcerer would never come. A few attempted to
ingratiate themselves with their new lord by attacking the
little band of Southerners; their bodies littered the granite
floor and Wolfsbane's axe dripped with their blood. The

wise majority poured into the outer tunnels in a wild dash for freedom. Caradoc and Arken rejoined their companions. Findhorn followed close behind, struggling under the weight of booty seized from the Wizard Lord's bedchamber: two immense volumes, a box of trinkets and talismans and an oddly adorned earthenware pot, presumably with some contents of interest to mages.

Wolfsbane and his little band were for remaining in the great chamber and polishing off the few Simians still patiently awaiting the return of their fallen master. As Findhorn pointed out, however, the task was accomplished and he would not return. Without him they faced an enemy without a purpose; the wandering bands of Simian brigands that might threaten their villages in the future would be no match for the organised peoples of the Southmoor, and who could tell, Simians were innocent and uncorrupted once, they might be so again. They should all feel thoroughly proud of themselves, some even more than others, he had said with a genial wink in the direction of Caradoc and Ellie, and could all go home.

The badgers grumbled discontentedly but no one else needed persuading. They joined the dwindling band of Simian refugees along the path to the outside world.

No light reached the inner chambers of the former realm of the Wizard Lord from the world beyond and as they bore down upon the mouth of the tunnel they had no idea of the time of day. Even as they emerged into the outside world they were not much enlightened. It was undoubtedly daytime but whether early morning, noon or dusk was anyone's guess. For they gazed out upon a world of water. An immense and opaque curtain of grey rain hung between heaven and earth as if to obscure the drama of Hangingstone Hill from the happier lands beyond. Not content with shedding their contents upon the land it seemed that the clouds themselves had settled softly and snugly on the moorland hills without the least intention of ever moving on. The air itself dripped and oozed, porous and spongelike, and from the mossy slopes on which they stood there bubbled up little rivulets of cool, clear spring water.

Caradoc surveyed the scene with feelings of elation. Beyond the great watery veil surrounding Hangingstone Hill there would be other veils, sweeping away in flamboyant waves across the torscape, dancing down the escarpment of the Northmoor across the dripping yellow gorse bushes to the gentler tors of the south and away beyond the moors over the valleys of the land of little rivers to the great sea. The rain would cleanse the land, washing away the sordid wicked works of the enemy. And when the rains were done and the clouds lifted, the great menace that had threatened the peaceful Moorlander villages of the Southmoor would be utterly gone. He gulped back cleansing tears of joy; he would never take the life of a young Moorlander for granted again.

Findhorn dispatched a rescue party into the valley: Fortinbras, who was keen for the opportunity to display some leadership, and Polycanthus. The captured workers in the dungeons under the hill would need to be brought the good news and the walls of their dungeons broken. The rest set out for home. They took the shortest route across the high moor towards Drizzlecombe, seeing no further need for caution. They made rapid progress but as they passed near the head of the sixth river, Bowerman's leg began to give cause for concern. Findhorn had examined the wound on a number of occasions and was bemused. It seemed to heal remarkably quickly; yet the more it healed the less control Bowerman seemed to have over the limb. It was a long summer's day and no one wished to stop whilst there was still light to travel by. Long before the dim light had failed, Bowerman could walk no more. They constructed a great stretcher and between them the two burliest badgers and the two burliest Moorlanders bore the immense frame of the Giganticus to the very edge of the Northmoor.

That night Caradoc slumbered peacefully for the first time in many days, dreaming of his mother, his friends and whortleberry pie – all were but a few days away. He awoke early to a clear, perfect sky. The rains had done their work and returned to the sea. He had bedded down at the southern edge of the camp, perhaps feeling subconsciously that he slept a little closer to Drizzlecombe and home. He strolled towards the nearby escarpment edge and cast his eyes southwards. It seemed that he could see beyond the moor itself, beyond the land of little rivers to the sea – a silver ribbon at his vision's edge. Only a few weeks before he had stood on the banks of the second river gazing northwards at the vast lowering mass of the Northmoor – perhaps at the very spot on which he now stood. Then it had seemed the abode of demons and ghouls. Now it teemed with every form of moorland life. Green grasshoppers chirped unseen in the heather, skylarks chattered frenetically on high and tiny blue butterflies fluttered gorgeously from grassy turf to grassy turf like little floating flakes of fallen sky. The Northmoor was alive again.

Caradoc turned to find a friend to share the experience. The camp was strangely empty. He wandered back through the scattered belongings of his friends. Beyond a small hillock at the edge of the camp he spied his father's head and beside it that of Brand. He skipped excitedly to meet them and ran around the hillock, straight into the arms of Polycanthus. His face was flecked with tears. Caradoc looked beyond him. Upward of thirty souls sat in the depression beyond the hillock. All stared in stunned, sorrow-laden silence at the body of the fallen Giganticus, still stretched upon the sturdy bed they had built him but now utterly bereft of life. Despite the frantic efforts of Findhorn the malady that had taken hold of the injured limb had spread remorselessly through his body and just as the summer sun had peeped above the moorland's eastern rim, Bowerman's life was finally lost.

To Caradoc it seemed inconceivable that a creature so immeasurably strong could be vanquished by so innocuous a wound. He did not doubt that some final devilish trickery of the Wizard Lord had done its work. He felt rage as much as grief. Struggling vainly to hold back bitter tears Caradoc ran blindly through the camp back to the same spot from which he had looked out upon the world so optimistically only a few moments past. Now he felt only the blackest of despair. He sat down on a flat granite slab at the point where the ground fell away most sharply. He felt that if he only leant forward a foot or so he would pitch head first into the ravine far below.

After a few moments his father sat down alongside him, followed closely by Findhorn.

"He died to save the moor," his father said warmly. "He would have wanted us to remember him that way."

"But why did he have to die?" demanded Caradoc with the precarious logic of grief. "Just when everything seemed so perfect. Why can things never turn out perfectly?"

No one replied as no one knew the answer. Caradoc had not really expected an answer to that question but he did to the next.

"But how did he die? He seemed perfectly alright after he fought the giant Simian."

"The wound itself was not serious," replied Findhorn, relieved that the conversation had moved on to less metaphysical matters. "But the blade was poisoned, by some concoction of the Wizard Lord's. Monkshood, I think, and something else. Had I been at home I might have saved him – an antidote might have been possible. But there was no time. Its course was swift and its working pernicious. I could do nothing to help him."

These last words were uttered with a tone of dark despair surpassing even Caradoc's doleful mood. Arken flailed around for some suitable words of consolation but could think of nothing.

They sat glumly and silently for a moment. Caradoc then broached a subject that had played much on his mind. "Was he really the last Giganticus?" he asked.

"I cannot say for certain," said Findhorn. "But he did not think so. He had heard stories of another on the moors beyond the southern seas – a relative, he thought. He spoke of travelling there but I am not so sure. Even when I was a boy there were very few. And other than Bowerman I have not heard tell of Gigantici for many a year. The world is changing," he continued. "The old peoples are dying. The future world will be a world of men."

Findhorn seemed to speak these words without the least idea of the effect they might have on his listeners. Caradoc's thoughts drifted back to that perilous night in the valley of the fifth river when he had first looked into the soft, sad eyes of the Giganticus and sensed a strange and intangible kinship which now at last he understood.

"He was just a big Moorlander, wasn't he?"

Findhorn did not reply.

"Are Moorlanders dying out too?" stammered Caradoc hesitantly, as if he did not really want to know the answer.

Findhorn saw that he must shake himself free from his own dejection and turn his attentions to the alleviation of the damage he had already done.

"We must all of us die," he said unconvincingly.

"Peoples as well as individuals. But there's no need to worry," he coaxed, "the noble race of Moorlanders will see out your days – and those of the numerous young Caradocs who will come after you, I shouldn't wonder."

Findhorn beamed encouragingly, and Caradoc and Arken both wrung out a smile.

All three gazed away across the Southmoor as if contemplating that far-off time when its hills and valleys would no longer nurture the little Moorlander villages that now nestled there snug and unseen. Their reverie was interrupted by a hearty bellow from Fortinbras.

"There you are, we've been looking for you everywhere. Come on, we must make Drizzlecombe by dusk."

Caradoc sprang up excitedly, followed immediately by Arken. They had not eaten well for days and the reputation of the Drizzlecombe table was second only to that of Buzzard Woods. Caradoc wondered if his mother would be there to greet him.

"Make it by dusk? We'll make it by teatime!" exclaimed Caradoc. "Come on, let's run all the way."

Findhorn only did not move.

"Here is where we must part," he said slowly. "If only for a while."

"Why? Surely you're coming with us?" said Arken. "We've done our job, done it perfectly. Now we can go home and rest."

"You can go home and rest. But I have another job to do, one I did not know about when we started out."

"Where are you going?" asked Caradoc, crestfallen.

"I am going north, after the Sorcerer, to free or kill his captive if he is not already dead. I cannot allow him to suffer at the hands of Magog."

Even the garrulous Caradoc was dumbfounded. The next question positively demanded to be asked, but Findhorn did not wait for him to do so.

"You will no doubt wonder why," he said with

admirable understatement, "I should risk my life for one who has done us nothing but evil but he was not evil once. Once he was a mischievous, innocent, loving boy running in the valleys of the Southmoor – much as you do today, Caradoc. His only vices, if they be such, were an excessive curiosity and intelligence, also much like you, and perhaps an overhealthy pride in his own abilities.

"But then war came, a war whose history I have already related to your moot. And war changed the life of this young boy utterly, as it changed the lives of many. He was separated from his family, most of whom he never saw again. He became a prisoner in a city of slaves. He saw the power that goes with great knowledge untempered by mercy. Such was his curiosity and intelligence that he began to absorb the skills of his teacher. He became the star pupil. So complete was his mastery of his mentor's arts that eventually and inevitably his mind harboured ambition and treachery. By means of his master's most potent toxins the star pupil set himself up in his master's place."

"The Wizard Lord, you obviously mean the Wizard Lord," interrupted Caradoc at what seemed an appropriate point. "But you speak as if you knew him."

"I did," replied Findhorn emotionally, "he was my youngest brother."

Since his first meeting with Findhorn, Caradoc had become accustomed to the unexpected; but this latest revelation beggared belief and for a moment Caradoc did not believe it. Findhorn was an old man. He had been through much. Perhaps he rued the passing of the old world even more deeply than Caradoc. Perhaps his fabled judgement was at last deserting him.

His father had no such doubts. "When did you realise?" he asked. "Surely you have not known for long."

"You're right. I haven't," Findhorn replied. "I did not know for certain until last night. Until very recently I had no inkling whatsoever. Naturally like many I had speculated on the origins of the new Lord of the Northmoor and on his sudden rise to power. I knew he was no issue for Magog, for rumour said he was human. Whatever ancient forgotten race spawned the evil of Magog himself, neither history nor rumour has left record – but he was certainly not human. I assumed that all my family had died in the Great War – or had fled beyond the seas. I had no hope that I would meet with any of my kin again.

"When I first looked into the face of the Wizard Lord before our dear friend slew the giant Simian, I sensed familiarity. Whether he did also I cannot tell. But even then I did not guess at the reason. When we fled from his private chambers I took with me some artefacts and two volumes. I took the latter in the vague hope that I might learn something of value from them, although I was not fully resolved even to open them. Others had been seduced by a too-complete mastery of Magog's art. I lacked full confidence in my own will to resist.

"But when last night I finally realised that our friend's salvation was beyond my present means and knowledge, I hoped that I might find enlightenment in the stolen volumes. They might hold the secret of the ingredients of the venom, even if they did not contain its antidote.

And an understanding of its creation would surely lead me to the source of its undoing, as nature provides a complementary good to each of its various evils. I had only to find it."

Here Caradoc found much that positively demanded explanation; but now at least he would not distract the teller from his tale. Findhorn continued.

"The first volume was of little use, written in some dark script that I could not decipher, perhaps the work of Magog or one of his people. But the second volume was in the common tongue. I understood it and what was more I had read it before. It was my father's book. I realised in a flash how it had come to be here and who had brought it: my brother, my youngest brother... my favourite brother. It seemed to me then inconceivable that I had not recognised him before. And so as I have said, I have another job to do."

Caradoc pondered for a moment on the bloody means Magog might employ to take his vengeance. He did not doubt that the Sorcerer had skills enough to inflict an eternity of suffering. He had no brother himself but he knew that any attempt to dissuade Findhorn from the course he had outlined would be futile.

"Must you go immediately?" said his father who had obviously reached the same conclusion. "I thought that the release of Magog from the effects of the white angel fungus was only temporary?"

"So it is," replied Findhorn. "The fungus will reclaim him again but how soon I cannot say and therefore I must go and help my brother. Our good friend Windhover is tracking his course for me but a moorland buzzard does not like to stray far beyond the edges of the moor and he will return soon. I know the course my quarry has taken but if I am not hot upon his trail before he descends below the northern escarpment I may lose him. So, this is farewell – for a little while."

"But when will you teach me the common tongue?" Caradoc complained. "I've learnt so little."

"There will be time for that," Findhom replied reassuringly. "I hope to meet with you at Buzzard Woods before the evenings lengthen."

Findhorn was inept at farewells; they embarrassed him. He would slip away to the east, avoiding the camp and awkward words. He shuffled backwards as if to make his escape but Caradoc would not let him off the hook so easily. Skipping across the boulders he sprang onto the old man's shoulders and hugged him for all he was worth. Tears welled in the Mage's eyes as he buried his head in the proffered shoulder, obscuring his emotion from the world. Then after a few moments he gently slipped free from Caradoc's grasp and was gone. Caradoc thought that he caught one last glimpse of his lonely, hunched figure twenty minutes later or so as the group moved away over the boggy land to the south of the southern escarpment – a speck of grey moving slowly along the northern skyline, but he could not be sure; it might even have been a refugee Simian.

The journey to Drizzlecombe took no longer than expected despite the formidable burden of their dead friend and as the rim of the setting sun nestled snugly against the hills of the western moors, the company gazed down upon it once again. Polycanthus had jogged on ahead to warn the villagers of their arrival and as the company passed down the valley of the second river the entire inhabitants poured out to meet them. Caradoc immediately picked out his mother and so delighted was he to see her that even kisses in the presence of Bluffinch and Ellie could be tolerated. Rollo and Michaelmas were there, as were many of the older Moorlanders; even the venerable Ambergris and Ebenezer had made the journey. Potentilla was with them and he wondered how many Moorlanders knew of the crucial part she had played in their deliverance. Turmeric was there too − his father's old friend who had vanished with the Grimspound settlers. He felt delighted for his father; no doubt Turmeric too had a tale to tell.

They buried Bowerman that evening before the light failed, beneath a great granite mound above the western bank. From there, so future Moorlander generations believed, their ancient protector looked down upon their villages with a watchful eye. Their senior elder, Ambergris the Grey, spoke at his funeral − spontaneously and eloquently as only Ambergris could. He spoke of a new life awaiting the moor, cleansed of the corruption which had threatened to pollute it utterly. An age of men, and of Moorlanders too, not old ones like himself but those young ones who had done so much to save their dear moor. Bowerman had symbolised the age that had passed − an age of honour and selflessness. He had loved life but he was prepared to die to ensure that these qualities survived into the new age; and with his death he had secured for the moor a new life.

After Ambergris had finished speaking his audience stood in silence for some minutes before the burial cairn. Then in little groups they drifted back to the village. Arken and Caradoc remained alone on the bank above the mound. It was mid evening and the little light that remained was hurrying over the western rim of the world to brighten the lands beyond.

Arken clapped his arm firmly around his son's shoulder. "Well, it now really is over," he said cheerfully.

"But Ambergris says it's just beginning," said Caradoc doubtfully. "He isn't so wise after all... is he?"

Arken looked at him querulously but said nothing.

"He isn't wise because he doesn't know that Bowerman was a Moorlander – and that we are part of the old age, just like he was."

Caradoc saw his father smile.

"You worry too much," he replied. "You think too much. Nobody lives forever. Remember what Findhorn said. You have a whole life to look forward to, so enjoy it and stop worrying."

The smell of roast boar drifted up the valley and mingled with the sound of laughter and impending revelries.

"And you'd better start enjoying it now," he chuckled.

Caradoc did not know whether Ambergris was wise or not... but his father certainly was; and arm in arm they bounded off towards the village and the warm welcoming smiles of his old friends Rollo and Michaelmas and his new friends Ellie and Bluffinch, to feast as only Moorlanders know how.